"Look… I should h
sooner." Emmy sw

She was biting her lip in a way that was making warning bells ring loudly inside his head, when suddenly she sat up, all that hair streaming down over her shoulders like liquid gold. She looked like a goddess, he thought achingly, when her next words drove every other thought from his head.

"You have a son, Kostandin."

What she said didn't compute. In fact, she'd taken him so completely by surprise that Kostandin almost told her the truth. That he'd never had a child, nor wanted one. His determination never to procreate was his get-out-of-jail-free card. He felt the beat of a pulse at his temple. Because what good was a king without an heir?

Sharon Kendrick once won a national writing competition by describing her ideal date: being flown to an exotic island by a gorgeous and powerful man. Little did she realize that she'd just wandered into her dream job! Today, she writes for Harlequin, and her books feature often stubborn but always to-die-for heroes and the women who bring them to their knees. She believes that the best books are those you never want to end. Just like life...

Books by Sharon Kendrick

Harlequin Presents

Secrets of Cinderella's Awakening
Confessions of His Christmas Housekeeper
Her Christmas Baby Confession
Innocent Maid for the Greek
Italian Nights to Claim the Virgin
The Housekeeper's One-Night Baby

Jet-Set Billionaires

Penniless and Pregnant in Paradise

Passionately Ever After...

Stolen Nights with the King

Visit the Author Profile page
at Harlequin.com for more titles.

The King's Hidden Heir

SHARON KENDRICK

HARLEQUIN®
PRESENTS™

Recycling programs
for this product may
not exist in your area.

ISBN-13: 978-1-335-59335-1

The King's Hidden Heir

Copyright © 2024 by Sharon Kendrick

All rights reserved. No part of this book may be used or reproduced in any
manner whatsoever without written permission except in the case of brief
quotations embodied in critical articles and reviews.

This is a work of fiction. Names, characters, places and incidents
are either the product of the author's imagination or are used fictitiously.
Any resemblance to actual persons, living or dead, businesses, companies,
events or locales is entirely coincidental.

For questions and comments about the quality of this book,
please contact us at CustomerService@Harlequin.com.

TM and ® are trademarks of Harlequin Enterprises ULC.

Harlequin Enterprises ULC
22 Adelaide St. West, 41st Floor
Toronto, Ontario M5H 4E3, Canada
www.Harlequin.com

Printed in Lithuania

MIX
Paper | Supporting
responsible forestry
FSC® C021394

The King's
Hidden Heir

For my darling husband, Pete Crone—an exemplar
of humour, adventure and romance. xxx

CHAPTER ONE

London

HIS BODY WAS bathed in the sheen of the early-morning sun. Every sinew washed with pale gold. A powerful thigh spread carelessly over her hip, anchoring her where she most wanted to be.

With him.

Next to him.

And—at countless points throughout the night—under him.

Her body still warm with the aftermath of pleasure, Emerald's gaze drifted over him, drinking in all that hard muscle and marvelling that a man could be so strong and so beautiful.

'I'm not asleep.'

His accented voice filtered through the air and she blushed, unsure of how to respond, because she'd never done anything like this before. Picking up the mechanics of sex was the easy bit—it was the emotional side which was tricky. Would it be so wrong to relay an unarguable fact? She sighed. 'That was fantastic.'

'Yes, it was,' he agreed.

She stroked her finger over his arm. 'Really?'

'Really.' There was a pause while he removed his leg from her body and suddenly a breath of air rippled in from the open window onto her exposed skin and made her shiver. 'But you should have told me.'

She thought about pretending she didn't know what he was talking about but his tone had suddenly become touched with ice and instinct warned Emerald that a man like this would have no desire for game-playing.

A man like this.

What did she know of a man like this? Very little really, apart from the glaringly obvious.

He was a royal prince. A billionaire hunk pursued by just about every woman with a pulse and yet it had been her he had chosen. It was still difficult to get her head around that. But she hadn't known or cared about his status when she'd first met him, when he'd handed her his exquisite cashmere coat and she'd given him a ticket in exchange, at the gentlemen's club where she put in a few hours here and there to supplement her meagre income. She had just looked into the sapphire glitter of his eyes and totally lost her heart. She hadn't shown it, of course. She wasn't *that* stupid.

'That I was a virgin, you mean?' she ventured cautiously.

'Well, I certainly wasn't referring to my surprise when your debit card bounced,' he said wryly.

Emerald wondered whether that was intended to demonstrate just how different their circumstances were—as if he needed to! But none of it was relevant. He'd already explained this wasn't going to morph into a relationship and she'd told him she didn't care. She'd even convinced herself that she meant it.

Because magic didn't come along very often, did it? And when you got the chance, you needed to grab it fast. So she had. She'd had the most blissful night of her life and now she was going to have to do the most grown-up thing of all and pretend she didn't want to see him again.

CHAPTER TWO

Northumberland, six years later

HIS FACE STARED back at her and just the sight of it was doing strange things to her heart. Twisting it with a pain Emerald hadn't expected to feel, not after six years. Making her mind spin with unwanted images as the screen illuminated his autocratic features. Golden-olive skin and hair as black as a raven's wing. Eyes like splinters of blue glass, courtesy of the powerful Greeks who had invaded his country half a millennium ago, though his sensual lips owed more to the Italians, who had arrived a few decades later.

Feeling as if she'd been punched in the solar plexus, she turned away from the computer as her sister came charging into the small kitchen of the house they shared.

'Have you seen the news?' Ruby demanded.

Emerald huffed out a sigh. A mug of cold tea stood in front of her, next to a slice of untouched toast, which should have been fairly explanatory, given how much she usually enjoyed her breakfast.

She looked up to meet her twin's worried gaze. 'Yes, of course I've seen the news,' she answered quietly. 'The

Internet is awash with it. I keep telling myself to turn it off, but somehow I can't seem to look away.'

'No. I get that. The question is, what are you going to do?'

Emerald swallowed as she studied Kostandin's image for the hundredth time and wondered if she would ever become immune to those arresting features.

'Emerald?' said Ruby urgently. 'Did you hear me? I said, what are you going to do?'

Did she actually have to *do* anything? Emerald wondered. Couldn't she just bury her head in the sand and pretend none of it had ever happened? After all, when he'd said goodbye to her on that unseasonably frosty English morning Kostandin had made it clear he had no intention of seeing her again. He hadn't been unkind, but he had certainly been very specific.

'Don't waste a second of your time thinking about me, Emerald. I'm not in the market for a relationship. Understand?'

Of course she had. He was a royal prince and she a humble cloakroom attendant—it was hardly a match made in heaven. Their one-night stand was obviously intended to be just that and she'd told herself she should be grateful for his honesty. But it seemed she had been naïve.

Because several days after their passionate liaison his elder brother had been killed in a hunting accident and Prince Kostandin had become King Kostandin of Sofnantis. That had been a lot to process—but what had happened next had provided the killer blow to her tentative plans. For, with almost indecent haste, and despite having told her he never intended to marry *anyone*, her handsome royal lover had wed his dead brother's fiancée and they were living happily ever after.

Or so she and the rest of the world had thought—judging by the saccharine-tinted photos of the couple, which were periodically released by the palace and which made Emerald flinch every time she saw them.

But no. The latest news reports were stark. The King and Queen of Sofnantis had recently undergone a quiet and 'amicable' divorce. Was there any such thing? she wondered. The couple had requested 'privacy' and there would be no further statement.

Emerald might have been able to absorb this news in peace and think about whether it should be allowed to impact on her future, but Kostandin was on an official visit to London. He was tantalisingly close, not locked in his glittering palace far away. Wasn't fate offering her a golden opportunity to do what she had intended to do all those years ago? What her conscience was urging her to do, even though she was absolutely dreading it.

Ruby's voice broke into her thoughts. 'If you want my advice, you'll give him a wide berth. He won't want to see you,' her sister added, with hurtful candour.

'No, I'm sure he won't. But that's irrelevant, surely. My feelings aren't really the issue here.' Emerald licked her lips. 'The point is that he has a son. A son he doesn't even know about and I think he has a right to know.'

'And what about your rights?' demanded Ruby. 'Don't your needs count for anything? He's a *king*, for heaven's sake—and one of the most powerful men in the world. He's already shown how heartless he could be by acquiring a wife just weeks after sleeping with you. If you just pitch up there with his son and heir, isn't there a chance…?' She paused, delicately. 'Isn't there a chance he could take Alek away from you?'

'Things don't work like that any more,' argued Emerald staunchly, but she could hear the sudden leak of fear into the words she was saying as much to convince herself as her sister. 'Women don't have their children snatched away by men just because they're powerful.'

'Don't they? Aren't you forgetting something, Emmy? Despite being one of the wealthiest men in the world—what's the one thing he hasn't got? The only thing money can't buy, which is extra important for a king. A son and heir. Don't you think he's going to look at Alek—who we both know is the cleverest and most handsome little boy in the whole world—and decide he wants him, no matter what lengths he has to go to in order to achieve that?'

'Aren't you jumping the gun?' questioned Emerald crossly. 'I don't have to take Alek with me. I was planning to go and see him on my own and work out the best way of telling him. Obviously if he seems like some kind of autocratic control freak, I'll walk away, leaving him none the wiser.'

'But I presume you wouldn't have slept with him in the first place if you'd thought he was unstable?'

Emerald wondered what Ruby would say if she confessed that she'd barely known him when she'd spent that unforgettable night in his arms. She hadn't exactly *lied* about her brief relationship with the devastatingly attractive prince, but she hadn't been particularly forthcoming, either. Wasn't the truth that she felt slightly ashamed of getting pregnant by a man with whom she'd shared little more than engaging banter whenever he came into the posh London club where she worked? Until the night when he'd taken her out for dinner and suddenly the sky had exploded with stars—and her foolish heart with it. She wasn't the first woman to have her head turned by a gorgeous man, nor to have to deal with the surprise pregnancy which had followed, and she wouldn't be the last. Yet though she shared her sister's reservations, she knew she had to tell Kostandin about his boy. She couldn't let this secret burn a hole in her heart for much longer, and didn't she owe it to Alek, too?

Getting close to him was going to be the difficult bit. He wouldn't be able to move around with the ease he had always prided himself on before acceding to the throne. She hovered her mouse over the screen until it reached the page which listed the King's official UK engagements. A state banquet in his honour at Buckingham Palace tonight. A parade of military cadets who were passing out from the Sofnantian Military Academy tomorrow, and security would be tighter than tight in both those places. Her gaze skimmed downwards, until she reached the part which read:

The King will be holding a private party at his old members' club, on London's Strand. The chairman of the Colonnade Club professed himself 'thrilled and honoured' that the monarch was revisiting one of his old haunts.

Quickly, Emerald shut down her computer and carried it upstairs, away from the searching stare of her sister.

The modest cottage she shared with her son and twin

was described as having three bedrooms, but even the most optimistic person would have listed hers as nothing more than a boxroom. Alek had the biggest room and Ruby the next biggest. But Emerald was fine with that. She was used to coming last in the pecking order, because she was the one who had thrown their lives into disarray with the unplanned birth of her son. Plus, she relied on her sister for help, though it was much easier now Alek was at school. She closed her eyes and imagined his beloved jet-dark head bent diligently over his books, but hot on this rush of maternal pride came a shiver of apprehension. Her son's life might be about to change out of all recognition, and suddenly she was scared.

Picking up her phone, she scrolled through numbers she hadn't used for years. The first she tried was out of service and nobody answered the second. But then a familiar female voice answered her third attempt.

'Emmy?' said the voice doubtfully. 'Is that you?'

'It sure is. How are you, Daisy?'

'I'm good. What the hell happened to you? One day you were there and the next you were gone… You disappeared like a puff of smoke!'

Emerald's heart began to race. She didn't want to answer questions like that, especially not now. Nobody had known she was pregnant when she'd left London and that was the way she wanted it to stay, at least for the time being. 'Oh, I decided to turn my back on the city and embrace country living, and it was cheaper for my sister and I to start our catering business in Northumberland,' she said truthfully. She hesitated. 'You're not still working at the Colonnade, by any chance?'

'Too right, I am. Got promoted, too. I'm in charge of the staff rota now.'

'No way!'

'Yeah.' There was a pause. 'We missed you, Emmy. All the punters loved you.'

And one punter in particular, thought Emerald— though she doubted he would have used the word *love* in any context other than sex. Or was she being unfair? Kostandin might have flirted with her, but she had flirted right back, hadn't she? If any boundaries had been crossed before they had tumbled into bed together—they had both been complicit in crossing them. She cleared her throat. 'Listen, I'm in London next week. It would be great to see you but…well, I'm a bit strapped for cash. I don't suppose there's any chance of me doing a shift at the club?'

There was a pause. 'There could be,' said Daisy, dipping her voice in the way people did when they were about to tell you something they shouldn't. 'Remember that hunky prince who was a member here before he became a king?'

A mocking face and a hard body swam into Emerald's mind. A powerful thigh slung carelessly over her naked hip. She swallowed. 'Vaguely.'

'Well, he's throwing a big do here. A sort of trip down memory lane, I guess. And he's invited some of the members. We could do with an extra pair of hands for that. Someone we can trust. I can't really organise a last-minute booking through an agency—not when I'm dealing with an actual member of a royal family.'

Emerald's throat thickened, because this kind of opportunity seemed almost too good to be true. Had her luck changed for once—giving her relatively free access to a heavily guarded king?

'I'd really appreciate that,' she said huskily. 'I owe you, Daisy.'

'Sure. Look, why don't you come here around about five on Saturday afternoon and I'll fix you up with a uniform?'

Kostandin glanced around at the mass of people thronging in the columned reception room of his old members' club, each one of them trying to catch his eye. Had it been a mistake to come back? he wondered grimly. To imagine that he might somehow capture a sense of the man he used to be. Because wasn't it here, in London, that he had sampled a tantalising taste of freedom, before the constrictions of royal responsibility had been straitjacketed onto his unwilling shoulders?

He thought back to a lifestyle which now seemed like a distant dream. Those heady days when he'd been able to move around the world with relative anonymity, for he had worn his title lightly. And why wouldn't he, when he had never been intended to rule? The business he had built up through his own endeavours had paid dividends—and his development of induction motors had made him one of the wealthiest men on the planet. And when people enquired why he considered it necessary to work so hard, when his birthright would surely have provided a much easier option, he had shrugged, allowing them any amount of unfounded guesswork.

Because Kostandin knew the truth. He had seen his father ruined by emotional weakness and his brother corrupted by greed and excess. From the get-go it had been a point of honour for him to make his own way in the world, rather than benefit from the supposedly swollen coffers of his royal homeland. He hadn't wanted to be like them—and he hadn't been. Until a cruel fate had intervened and the powerful magnet of royal duty had sucked him back into the fold.

He glanced around, looking at the marble pillars which had given the historic London club its name. The famous establishment provided a discreet base for the wealthy and the well connected, but for Kostandin it was more than a place where you could meet on neutral territory, without fuss. Because it was here that he had met *her*—a woman who had blown away his mind and his body and made him behave so uncharacteristically. Before Emerald, he had only ever associated with women from a similar social stratum—it was easier that way. But he had allowed the foxy cloakroom attendant to disrupt his rigidly compartmentalised life to give him the most sensational night he could remember.

The sassy little blonde who had turned out—unbelievably—to be a virgin.

A virgin.

His body began to harden as he remembered their blissful encounter, when she had offered him her delicious body with a sweet fervour unlike anything he'd ever encountered. He had warned her about his boundaries and she had solemnly accepted them. The fact that he had taken her innocence had briefly haunted him, though he'd wondered if his faint flicker of conscience had simply been a way of justifying his uncharacteristic behaviour. But memories of the curvy little blonde stubbornly lingered, and hadn't he secretly fantasised about another night of no-strings sex with her, to help ease his aching body?

Wasn't that one of the reasons why he'd chosen this venue?

His private secretary, who had been glued to his side all evening, now made a quiet observation. 'Miles Buchanan and his wife are over there, Your Majesty, and I know they are eager to meet you. You remember, they recently donated a significant sum to your foundation.'

'Yes, yes,' said Kostandin, trying not to sound impatient—because why bother holding this party in the first place if he failed to keep his own boredom at bay? 'Bring them over.'

'At once, Your Majesty.'

Kostandin watched the diplomat making his way towards the attractive couple who were drinking in the corner, but he remained so preoccupied with his thoughts that the voice behind him barely registered and it wasn't until he heard the sound of a woman clearing her throat and saying, 'Excuse me, Your Majesty', that he came back to the present with a start.

Composing his face into the faintly forbidding mask he'd been forced to adopt since news of his divorce had become public—because women on the hunt for a royal husband were nothing if not determined—he prepared to rebuff the unwanted attention of someone who was breaking royal protocol by approaching *him* first. But the cool dismissal died on his lips as he found himself looking into a heart-shaped face and a pair of wide green eyes. At first he thought his mind was playing tricks on him—that his erotically nostalgic thoughts had conjured up an apparition. But then his gaze registered hair of a startling hue. The colour of corn, and sunshine. Thick and silky, it was piled into a neat knot on top of her head but he remembered it best spread over his chest, making it easy for him to weave his fingers through the voluminous strands and pull her face to his, and to…to…

'You,' he said, without thinking—and that in itself was strange, because didn't he usually measure every word he uttered, knowing that the language of kings was analysed for every nuance?

'Good evening, Your Majesty.'

She held her tray towards him but he paid the brimming glasses no heed, his attention caught by the crisp white shirt and form-fitting black skirt which clothed her petite body. Yet the stark monochrome uniform did nothing to disguise the luscious swell of her breasts, or the earthy femininity she exuded. It never had done, he realised achingly as he remembered anchoring those hips with his palms and sliding slowly into her incredible tightness. His heart slammed as he felt the urgent clamour of a hunger he'd denied himself for too long.

'Emerald,' he said abruptly.

'Whew!' A look of relief passed over her face. 'You remembered my name.'

'It wasn't exactly difficult,' he answered acidly, trying

to dampen down the powerful shaft of desire which was throbbing at his groin. 'You're wearing a name badge.'

'So I am.' A hint of colour rose in her creamy cheeks as he dragged his eyes away from her lapel.

'And it's a very unusual name,' he observed quietly.

'So is Kostandin,' she said, just as quietly.

It was a definite breach of protocol to call him that in public and all it did was reinforce the reason why she felt she had the right to do so. As their gazes clashed and her cheeks grew even pinker, Kostandin knew the kindest thing to do would be to dismiss her as graciously as possible. He was no longer the same man who had flirted with her every time he saw her in that little cubbyhole they called the cloakroom. And certainly not the same man who had removed her panties with his teeth and made her giggle with exultation. Perhaps she needed a gentle but diplomatic reminder that things were very different now that he was King.

And perhaps he needed to heed that reminder himself. At least, until the time was right.

Because he shouldn't be at the mercy of his senses like this. Hadn't he wondered whether his almost primitive desire for her might have lessened? Because that was clearly not the case. Yet it was no longer appropriate to associate with a woman like her, he told himself fiercely. *It never had been, really.* But suddenly his reservations seemed to crumble away. Hadn't he spent too long denying himself the things other men took for granted, in pursuit of an archaic form of duty? Why shouldn't he catch up with her, for old times' sake if nothing else?

'I'm surprised you're still here,' he observed. 'Weren't you talking about getting out of London at some point?'

'Yes, I was.' Long lashes blinked over her incredible eyes. 'I'm surprised you remember that.'

'Oh, you'd be amazed at how much I remember, Emerald,' he informed her softly. 'How about you?'

He saw her eyes darken. Saw the sudden parting of her lips, which reminded him all too vividly of things he'd tried his best to forget. The touch of her skin and the way she had licked at him until he had spilled his seed inside her mouth. The incomparable sensation of being deep inside her as she cried out his name with uninhibited joy. With her, sex had felt so different and he'd never been able to work out why.

'I'm sure I could easily match your powers of recall, given the chance,' she answered.

'Is that so?' he challenged.

Her eyes darkened with complicit fire and Kostandin's pulse began to hammer, as he began to make excuses for what he was about to do. Surely his whole life shouldn't be spent as a servant to destiny. He stared at a bright strand of blonde hair which had escaped from her hair clip to curve over one smooth cheek. Despite her lowly status, Emerald Baker had proved herself as discreet as he would wish any woman to be and their red-hot night had gone undetected. There had been no hints dropped to any newspaper columnists eager for a royal story—a scoop which would have been extra-controversial in light of his subsequent marriage. The tiny blonde had been the perfect candidate for their brief and very satisfying liaison.

His mouth dried.

How simple it would be to see if she was up for a repeat performance. No promises made. No hearts broken. Two grown-ups who knew what they wanted. Out of the corner of his eye he could see Lorenc making his way towards them and knew he had to act quickly.

'Emerald—'

'Would you like a drink, Your Majesty?' she said politely, extending her tray towards him, as if she had suddenly remembered what she was supposed to be doing.

'No. Not now.' He shook his head—the faintest elevation of his finger silently warning his private secretary not to approach. 'And certainly not here. I'd forgotten just how bad the wine could be.'

'The wine committee would be mortified to hear you say that.'

'But we could meet afterwards,' he continued impatiently. 'Would you like that—or do you have somewhere else you need to be?'

He saw the pleasure which flashed through her extraordinary eyes but it was tempered by something else. Something he couldn't quite compute. Kostandin frowned, but the luscious lines of her lips distracted him from his momentary sense of disquiet.

'No, I'd love that,' she answered. 'In fact—'

With an impatient wave of his hand, he cut her off. 'I have people I need to talk to,' he said abruptly. 'What time do you finish?'

There was a pause. 'I knock off at eleven.'

Kostandin's eyes narrowed as he glanced over at the ornate grandfather clock which predated the club's inception. No way was he hanging around here waiting for her—he had never waited for a woman in his life and didn't intend to start now. He could ask for the library upstairs to be made available and catch up on some of the state papers until she finished her shift. What was it the English said? To kill two birds with one stone.

'My car will be waiting for you at the back of the building. But let's keep it as low-key as possible.' His voice grew silky. 'We don't want to announce our assignation to the world, do we?'

'No, of course we don't,' she said brightly, but he couldn't help noticing that the glasses on her tray were jangling as she quickly turned away, almost as if her hands were trembling.

CHAPTER THREE

EMERALD'S PULSE WAS hammering as she emerged from the staff entrance at the back of the club and spotted the darkly gleaming limousine parked in the shadows, with another car close behind—presumably containing Kostandin's bodyguards. She'd gone through an agony of indecision as she'd changed out of her uniform, wondering if she should have agreed to this late-night meeting, or whether she should have asked to see him in the cold light of day. But most likely he would have refused, because it would have been inappropriate to expect such an important man to fit in with *her* plans. And what would she have suggested anyway, if he had agreed to see her? Arranged to meet him in some anonymous coffee bar or pub? His bodyguards would never have allowed it.

No. Better to get it over with and try not to get distracted. She wasn't here to flirt with him, no matter how easily she seemed to have slotted straight back into that role. Calm and collected was what she should be aiming for. But her mouth was dry as she made her way towards the car, wobbling slightly in her sister's sky-high heels, which she had insisted she borrow. 'Because you can't wear a pair of frumpy trainers if you're going to London to see the King,' Ruby had announced, her blunt statement only adding to the butterfly flutter of Emerald's nerves. 'In fact, you'd better have one of my dresses, too.'

But Emerald had resisted borrowing anything else, because Ruby was fashionable and she was not. And it was important not to feel any more of an imposter than she already did. As a working mum she usually dressed for comfort and tied her long hair back in a plait but tonight, as instructed, she had left it loose, at Ruby's bidding. 'Work it, Emmy—it's your best feature.' Maybe it was, but unfortunately it was now flapping around her face in this unseasonably cold wind and her best jumper and skirt made her look as if she were going on a job interview.

Yet despite all her misgivings, the evening had gone better than expected. It had been the King who had suggesting meeting up afterwards, not her. She hadn't needed to drop any heavy hints, or grovel, or risk getting turned down. Or—worst of all—blanked. That had been her biggest fear, that he wouldn't have a clue who she was. He *had* recognised her, which had come as a huge relief, but Emerald was still scared. Scared of what he might say and how he might react to what she was about to tell him. Scared, too, of the way he could make her feel. Even now. How could a body which she had neglected for six long years, suddenly burst into provocative life like this? Her breasts hadn't stopped aching since the moment Kostandin glanced down at her name badge and then glanced up to meet her heated gaze. How did he manage to make her feel that way with nothing more than a few clipped words and a mocking look?

Sometimes she'd wondered if time might have made her immune to his appeal, but she had got her answer tonight. If anything, he seemed even more charismatic. *That was because he was,* she reminded herself. Power was an aphrodisiac and he had power to burn. These days, he possessed absolute authority over his country and that, coupled with his dark good looks—made him even more irresistible.

When he'd swept into the ballroom at the Colonnade tonight, the whole room had grown silent. Men and women had been assessing him with hungry or openly curious eyes. But Emerald couldn't help thinking how *different* he'd seemed. He looked the same and yet it was hard to recognise him as the same man. In repose, his eyes were cold, his mouth tight and unforgiving. It was as though he was encased in a brittle exterior—as if his new title had cut him off from the rest of the world. As she made her way across the cobblestones where the chauffeur was holding open the passenger door and she slid onto the back seat, Emerald thought how unreal this felt. Of course it did. She was about to inform a powerful king that he had a son. But she needed to choose her moment carefully and that moment wasn't now. Not when Kostandin was seated so close to her on the plush leather seat, his long legs sprawled in front of him, his features shadowed as he turned to look at her. As she met the narrowed glitter of his eyes, Emerald vowed not to be intimidated. She needed to cling onto her sense of self and be strong, because those were her only assets.

'You came,' he observed softly.

'Did you think I wouldn't?'

He smiled. 'No.'

'Because women don't turn down the offer of a date with a man like you, I suppose?'

'I wasn't aware this was a date.' His gaze became mocking, as if he had noted her sudden rise in colour. 'I was referring to the fact that people are fairly predictable whenever they're dealing with a member of the royal family. And having invitations turned down is something which, frankly, never happens.'

Emerald nodded, trying to shake off her embarrassment and remember the type of thing she would have said back in the day, when she'd had nothing to lose. 'Should I feel sorry for you?'

His lazy smile widened. 'You can feel anything you want to feel, Emerald,' he returned softly. 'We both know that.'

It seemed that their intimate verbal shorthand was still intact and, oh, didn't it feel good? Briefly, Emerald closed her eyes. Because in the lonely nights which had followed their fling, she'd sometimes wondered if she had imagined this *thing* they had between them, or had embellished it to make herself feel better about what had happened.

Her breath caught in her throat as her eyelashes fluttered open to meet his molten gaze and she actually thought he was going to lean over and kiss her. But he didn't. Stupid to feel a crashing feeling of frustration. Not sensible at all. More importantly, she was allowing herself to be distracted and maybe this was as good a time as any to tell him. 'Kostandin—'

But the disembodied sound of the chauffeur's voice interrupted her, filtering through the intercom and speaking in a language she didn't understand. 'Damn,' Kostandin said softly, after a moment or two.

'What's wrong?'

'The paps are waiting.'

'But you must have known that might happen,' she said reasonably. 'After all, the papers published a list of your engagements.'

'Ah, but I wasn't expecting to have a passenger with me,' he observed, his shuttered gaze flicking over her. 'Especially a beautiful, unknown blonde with the ability to send the speculating press into overdrive.'

Beautiful. He had called her beautiful. Emerald forced herself not to get too excited by the throwaway compliment. 'So what's going to happen? Do you want me to get out and take a bus?'

'Don't be ridiculous,' he said. 'You'll need to duck, that's all.'

She looked at him blankly. 'Duck?' she echoed, puzzled.

'I'm not talking about the feathered variety they used to serve in that disgusting orange sauce at the Colonnade—'

'You're so critical of the club, Kostandin, it makes me wonder why you ever bothered being a member there.'

'Perhaps because it had plenty of other things going for it,' he purred.

'Oh?' She knew she was flirting with him but she couldn't seem to help herself. 'Such as?'

'Well, there's its prime position in the centre of London, for a start,' he said, deadpan.

'Yes, of course. There is that. And its easy access to the park, of course.'

'Of course.' His eyes glittered as he shot a narrow-eyed glance to the road ahead. 'What I mean is you're going to have to lie down on the back seat when we leave the club. It's the only way to avoid the cameras. But if the idea doesn't appeal, we could part now. I can have one of my back-up cars drop you off home, wherever that might be. Or you could stick to the original plan and come to the Sofnantis Embassy for a glass of champagne.' The challenge of his smile mocked her. 'Depends how much you want my company.'

She wanted his company very much—but not for the reasons he probably imagined. 'Oh, very well,' she said, as if she could take it or leave it, but the flicker of triumph in his eyes told her she hadn't fooled him one bit as he tapped his fingers on the smoked-glass panel which divided them from the driver.

'Lose them,' he instructed tersely, before turning his gaze on her, his subsequent smile driving every other thought from her head. 'Treat it like a game,' he advised softly. 'It's the only way to survive this strange life of mine.'

'You mean you never really take it very seriously?'

He shook his head. 'It's a little more complex than that. But you have to take your fun where you can.' His eyes glittered. 'Ready?'

'Sure,' she said, because when he looked at her that way she honestly thought she might have agreed to anything. 'Why not?'

The car accelerated and the weird thing was that very quickly it *became* fun—which was the last thing Emerald would have expected in the circumstances. But then, she was more used to hard work than frivolity. She'd spent the last five years bogged down by nappies and routine and, as often as not, with worry. She'd scrimped and saved and juggled work and childcare. She'd baked cakes at night and juggled business plans while Alek was in bed and never, *never* seemed to get enough sleep. She saved all her pennies for her darling son and bought her clothes from charity shops. Sometimes she'd felt old before her time and she was damned sure she looked it, too. But this grown-up version of hide-and-seek felt curiously carefree—as if she was making up for some of the years she'd missed out on.

She crouched down, flattening her torso against her knees, dimly aware of the incandescent flash of bulbs outside the window, the yell of voices and sense of urgency as the car increased its speed.

'Are you comfortable?' he asked.

'Mmm… Blissfully. Can't you tell?'

He gave a short laugh. 'It shouldn't be too much longer.'

'Thanks for the reassurance.' She wriggled a bit.

'But won't they wonder why your lips are moving when you're supposedly alone in the car? They might think you're talking to yourself, or I suppose you could be rehearsing a speech?'

'I don't usually rehearse speeches at this time of night in the back of a car, Emerald,' he offered drily. 'Now stop distracting me, will you? I have a message from one of my aides which I need to deal with,' he told her sternly.

He was the one who'd started this conversation but she wasn't going to say so, not when her senses were so aroused by him. By everything, really. By the way they had slipped so easily into that light and teasing wordplay and the weird contradiction of feeling more relaxed with him than with any other man she'd ever met, despite his royal status and her being at the opposite end of the social pecking order.

She could smell leather and the subtle scent of sandalwood she had always associated with him, but most of all she was aware of his proximity. She had taught herself not to remember the intimacy she had experienced with him because the memory was unbearably bittersweet—but now it was impossible to keep those forbidden images at bay. How dangerously easy it was to recall the memory of his warm skin against hers. His hardness thrusting deep inside her. The way she had choked out her disbelieving joy when he'd made her come, over and over again.

And nothing had changed. She still wanted him, she realised—and that was a distraction she really didn't need. She had to stay focussed and remember why she was here. *The only reason she was here.* She closed her eyes and stayed motionless, until he brushed his fingertips over her shoulder—a featherlight touch which made her tremble and silently she cursed the sudden warm beat of blood to her breasts.

'It's okay, Emerald. You can get up now.'

Missing that brief physical contact, she sat up, smoothing down her mussed hair to gaze out of the window, but the only thing she could see was the red and white glare of slowly moving London traffic, bumper to bumper. 'Where have they gone?' she questioned, looking in vain for a swarm of paparazzi.

'We've lost them. My bodyguards deployed a decoy car. They're very good at doing that. Mind you, the press are remarkably easy to confuse.'

Emerald studied the set of his profile. 'Is it always like this?' she ventured curiously.

'The very nature of the job is bizarre and isolating.' He shrugged. 'But it's particularly bad at the moment.'

She forced herself to say it. To overcome the tight knot of hurt which was knotted in her stomach, reminding herself that of course he hadn't betrayed her. How could you betray someone you were never supposed to see again? 'Because of the divorce, I suppose?'

'You could say that.'

Emerald nodded, knowing that once she told him about Alek they were probably going to have these kinds of grown-up conversations all the time, during the 'civilised' handover which would take place on neutral territory. The polite small talk which meant nothing other than a useful disguise for the messy churn of emotion. She was dreading her perceived future of possible shared parenthood, but she'd better get used to the idea.

'Was it very bad?' she asked, in the kind of under-standing voice she'd heard TV therapists use.

'I don't want to talk about it.'

'No. No, of course not. It's none of my business.'

'You're right,' he snapped. 'It's not.'

Suddenly his voice had become hard and unfriendly and the implications of that troubled her. Did that mean he was hurting badly after his divorce? Had the love of his life shattered his heart? People said emotional pain was the worst kind of pain of all and Emerald could vouch for that. And now she was going to have to tell him something which had the potential to shatter his world even more—and she was dreading that, too.

Soon the luxury car was turning into one of the quiet side roads abutting Regent's Park—a pair of tall, wrought-iron gates opening and shutting behind them to enclose them in a shadowy, tree-lined compound where she could see the occasional flash of a torch and the gleam of a dog's eyes.

'Welcome to the Sofnantian Embassy,' Kostandin said.

Emerald scrambled out of the car and looked up at the Palladian mansion. 'Wow,' she said.

'You like it?'

Who wouldn't like it? she thought. But it was so *big*. So elegant. A different world, and a daunting environment in which to deliver her bombshell news. She'd never really glimpsed the royal side of his life before and as she stepped onto the gravel path, she suddenly felt out of her depth. 'Will there be er...servants?'

'That depends. If you want servants, I can have legions of them at your disposal. All the pomp and ceremony you require can be yours for the taking, Emerald,' he drawled. 'All you have to do is say the word.'

She wrinkled her nose. 'I'll pass on that if you don't mind.'

Kostandin successfully hid his surprise, because most people were turned on by the trappings of his ancient title and all the paraphernalia which went with it. The palaces. The jewels. And the power... That was the biggest turn-on of all.

But not for Emerald, he recalled. That side of him had never been part of the deal. She had known he was a prince, yes—but had treated him as a man. The night they'd spent together had been unplanned, but she had been content to spend it incognito. Their room at the Granchester Hotel had been fairly ordinary by his standards, probably because he'd told her to book it in her name. In fact, that had been the only blip during their brief encounter—when she'd confided that her debit card had been declined because she didn't have enough money in her account to pay for it. He remembered the way she'd flinched when he'd slid his credit card towards her, and for a moment he'd thought she was going to refuse it.

He led the way up the marble steps but, despite having instructed his private secretary to make no fuss, it was Lorenc who opened the door for them, his gaze falling with assessment on the tiny blonde. How would his private secretary view her? Kostandin wondered idly. Would he disapprove of the fact that her pale blonde hair was mussed and untidy from crouching down on the back seat of the car and perhaps jump to the conclusion that the King had been running his fingers through it?

If only.

Would he disapprove of her cheap little jumper and skirt, or shoes which were higher than the ones he remembered her wearing?

'Lorenc,' he said huskily, 'I'd like you to meet Emerald—'

'Baker,' she filled in quickly, as if she was worried he'd forgotten—which, in truth, he had. 'Though lots of people call me Emmy.'

'Indeed,' said his aide thoughtfully. 'Your face seems very familiar.'

'That's because it is,' she said chattily. 'I served you a drink at the Colonnade Club earlier. A tomato juice, as I recall—since you told me you never drank alcohol when you were working.'

Kostandin almost laughed out loud to see the expression on the other man's face because, like most diplomats, he disapproved of instant familiarity between strangers.

'I am delighted to make your acquaintance, Miss Baker,' Lorenc announced formally.

Kostandin held up his hand to truncate the laboured introductions. 'Just have some champagne brought up to the Plavezero suite, will you?' he said, turning to find the petite blonde sniffing at the lavish display of lilies which adorned the entrance hall. 'Are you hungry, Emerald?'

His use of her name seemed to startle her because as she drew away from the flowers and looked up, a dark flush entered her creamy cheeks. 'Er, no, thanks.'

Kostandin's heart missed a beat. Did she have any idea how enchanting she looked when she blushed like that? It made him think about his delicious discovery of her unexpected innocence and how his disbelief had turned into the most intense pleasure he'd ever experienced. Suddenly he found himself wondering how many men Emerald Baker had slept with in the intervening years, unprepared for the savage burst of jealousy which flooded through him. Her sexual history was irrelevant, he reminded himself. It was the present which mattered and he was eager to explore all the possibilities of that.

He ushered her into the Plavezero suite, which was named after his country's capital and studded with its most precious artefacts. Most of the furniture was crafted from the rare blackwood trees which grew in the northernmost forests of Sofnantis, and the cavernous space was softened by the faded hues of ancient silken rugs. It was an undeniably beautiful room, especially when lit by firelight flickering in the huge grate, as it was tonight. But Kostandin had never been dazzled by the accoutrements of royal life, even as a child.

Especially as a child.

He gave a bitter smile as he thought back to the chaos of the past, and the timeline which had brought him to this place. The monarchy he had accepted because there had been no other choice and which inwardly he had railed against, long into the nights which had followed. But he had done his duty. He had stepped up to the plate and embraced the concept of service. Under his reign, Sofnantis had entered a new and golden age—because he was a man who would accept nothing less than success.

But now the tank was empty and he had nothing left to give. He had played the sovereign role to the best of his ability, but his heart had never really been in the task. Many of his nation's cartoonists portrayed him as grim-faced and unsmiling, and in all honesty he couldn't disagree with them. Which was why things were going to change. And soon. He thought about his cousin. Didn't the people of Sofnantis deserve a ruler who actually *enjoyed* being King, instead of someone who saw the role as a burden?

But those plans were for another day. Tonight, he was going to put all that out of his head and focus on Emerald Baker. A servant entered the room with a tray of drinks, before noiselessly leaving. Kostandin gestured for Emerald to sit on one of the sofas but she shook her head, her expression suddenly clouding. She turned away from him, her shoulders set and tense—and although it was a massive breach of protocol to turn your back on a member of the royal household, and would have appalled Lorenc, Kostandin quickly sought to put her at ease.

'It's all a little overwhelming, I know,' he said. 'Rather too much clutter for my liking.'

She turned back to face him, her shoulders still tense. 'Kostandin,' she said.

There was an odd note in her voice, but he was too distracted by the fire-splashed fall of her hair to heed it. 'So few people call me by my first name any more,' he reflected.

'Because of your elevated position, I suppose?'

'Well, yes. There is that, of course.' He paused. 'But nobody ever says it the way you do.'

'Oh?' She looked startled. 'And how's that?'

'Seriously?'

White teeth dug into a soft bottom lip. 'Uh-huh.'

'Soft and sweet and tender.' He slanted her a mocking look as she blushed. 'You said it that way just before I kissed you for the first time.'

'D-did I? Fancy you remembering that.'

'Oh, I remember a lot about that night.' There was a pause and his voice grew husky. 'You were looking at me then, just like you're looking at me now...'

'How?' she whispered as his words tailed off.

'As if you wanted me to touch you. As if you were longing to have sex with me again.'

She drew in a sharp breath, his candour seeming to

surprise her—though nobody could have been more surprised by his words than himself.

'Or am I mistaken?' he questioned silkily.

CHAPTER FOUR

EMERALD FROZE AS Kostandin's silken question reverberated around the room. Even though that incredible chemistry was still fizzing between them, she hadn't expected him to come out and *acknowledge* it like that, as if talking about sex were as normal as talking about the weather. He was throwing down a challenge and she knew exactly how she should respond. Shut it down, right now. It was wrong on so many levels and her big secret was still burning a hole in her heart. She had come here to tell him about his son and that was supposed to be the only thing on her mind.

But when he looked at her like that. With hunger in his eyes, yes, but with something else, too. Something which flickered behind the darkening sapphire and resonated with the emptiness which had existed inside her for so long. He had implied that being crowned King had isolated him and she had witnessed that for herself. Amid all the celebratory hustle at the Colonnade Club tonight, he had seemed remote and apart from everyone else and here, in the magnificent setting of his embassy, he cut just as lonely a figure.

But the waves of desire radiating from his body were

almost tangible. All he was doing was subjecting her to that smoky stare and yet it was turning her on unbearably. Suddenly, it was difficult to breathe properly and the heat in her core was distracting. She could feel her nipples hardening beneath her blouse. And he had noticed. His eyes were fixed on the rapid rising and falling of her breasts and she saw the effort it took for him to drag his gaze away to study her face, his eyebrows raised in question.

Would it be so wrong to do this? she wondered achingly. Wouldn't it make telling him easier if they were as close as a man and woman could be, before she uttered words which would inevitably change both their lives? If she could remind him of the mutual pleasure they'd once shared and the wonderful if unexpected gift which had resulted from that passionate night together?

'No, you're not mistaken,' she said slowly.

He didn't move. His body was motionless as if it had been carved from marble and Emerald wondered if he was regretting his words—or maybe even preparing to retract them. But then he smiled and the slow curve of his lips was making her heart thunder.

'Come here,' he commanded softly.

In the breathless excitement of that moment, Emerald felt past and present blending together—like butter and sugar when you were mixing a cake. And suddenly she was back in that place where she'd felt curiously equal to him. Equal enough to answer back and make herself prolong this deliciousness for as long as possible—no matter how much her hungry body was urging her to rush straight into his arms. She met his heated gaze. 'And if I don't?'

'If you don't...' The gaze was growing more speculative by the second—filled with an incandescent blue fire which blazed through her. 'Then I might be forced to conclude that you'd like me to come over there and show you exactly how much I want you.'

Emerald blinked. It was the most unashamedly alpha statement she could have imagined, and it was turning her on even more. He might be a king, but in that moment he sounded more like a caveman and the contrast of that was irresistible. Perhaps she needed to approach this with caution and tell him there were things they needed to discuss first. But when you had denied yourself pleasure for as long as she had, rational thinking wasn't easy. In fact, it was darned near impossible, when your body was on *fire*.

She tilted her chin and her hair swayed against her back. 'Go ahead, then,' she said boldly. 'I'm not stopping you.'

He moved toward her, sinuous and graceful as a jungle cat, his dark gaze fixed on her. 'No, you're not, are you?' he murmured as he pulled her into his arms and that first sweet contact made her shiver. 'In fact, the light you're giving me right now is as green as your incredible eyes.'

Emerald felt dazed as he bent his head and touched his lips to kiss her—a kiss she'd never thought would happen again.

Her brain cleared.

Because he'd married another woman. He'd spent

the last five years living in a golden palace with Lul-
jeta, his beautiful, high-born queen, and presumably
had been kissing her just like this.

But even that cold swamp of reason wasn't enough
to make Emerald hold back, murmuring her approval
as he slid his tongue inside her mouth, and the intimacy
of that contact sent a wave of need jack-knifing through
her pelvis.

'Oh!' she gasped.

'You like that?'

'What do you think?'

'This is what I think,' he growled, levering her even
closer.

'Oh!' she gasped, for a second time, because now she
could feel the imprint of his erection straining against
the fine material of his suit and that blatant demon-
stration of his arousal sent her pulse-rate soaring even
higher. And all the while her core was melting. Her body
was growing liquid with need, and maybe she communi-
cated her frustration to him, because when she instinctively circled her hips in silent entreaty, he pulled his
mouth away from hers and gave a low laugh.

'Tell me what you want, Emerald,' he commanded
huskily. 'Tell me.'

'You!' she declared, the words rushing from her lips.
'I want you.'

And suddenly he was exploring her with urgent fingers. His palms were skating hungrily over the nipples
peaking beneath her sensible blouse, then moving down
to cup her buttocks, luxuriously kneading her fleshy
bottom.

'You're so tiny,' he growled as he started undoing her blouse, his long fingers making swift work of the buttons. He gave a husky moan of approbation as it fluttered open and he peeled it from her shoulders. And now he was sliding her skirt down over her hips, every touch of his fingers making her tremble. He was so gorgeous and she should have felt shy as she stood before him in nothing but her modest bra and pants, yet when he looked at her like that—his face tense with an almost savage hunger—she was filled with a sense of her own sexual power and an idea she couldn't shift.

That maybe this was meant to be.

Was it? she wondered as he tore off his own clothes and hurled them on top of hers. Was it possible that when she told him her news, he might actually receive it gratefully? He was isolated now, as King, but all that could change when he found out about Alek and realised how gorgeous he was. Ruby was right. He needed an heir. Who was to say they couldn't be a *family*? Princes met girls in bars and made them their princesses. Fairy tales happened sometimes, didn't they? *Didn't they?*

'Now let's get you out of this damned lingerie,' he growled, with hungry intent.

Which sounded like no fairy tale *she'd* ever read, but when he was making her feel like this—who cared?

'Yeah. Let's,' she agreed.

With unsteady fingers Kostandin unclipped a bra which was doing little to contain the magnificent breasts which spilled out into his waiting fingers like two pieces of ripe fruit. He sucked on an engorged nipple and heard her playful yelp before she bent her head to do the same to him. For a while he let her, but when her fingers tip-toed towards his groin, he reared back like an unbroken stallion. If she touched him there, he couldn't guarantee what would happen. Or rather, he could…

Kicking off his shorts, he freed his erection and her corresponding little gasp made him want to plunge straight into her. But one thing he never forgot, no matter how great the provocation, was protection. His mouth tightened. Because no child of his would ever be entering this world.

Retrieving a condom from his trousers, he put it within easy reach and sucked in a ragged breath as he gathered her in his arms. He felt so hard it was almost unendurable. But maybe that was understandable. It had been a long time. But even so. Was she intuitive enough to realise that nothing had changed?

'Tonight,' he groaned.

'Wh-what about it?'

'You know what this is, don't you, Emerald?' he demanded urgently. 'It's amazing but it's physical. That's all. Just like last time. Do you understand what I'm saying?'

His words were a warning, Emerald knew that—but it was one she had no intention of heeding. She couldn't seem to stop herself, especially now he had taken her knickers off. Her breasts felt heavy and tight. Her core was soft and thrumming. Because hadn't she longed for this, in those rare moments when desire had crept up on her unannounced—when she'd remembered that she was a woman, as well as a busy working mum?

'Yes, I understand,' she moaned as his hand slid between her thighs.

'You're wet like silk. Like honey. Like cream,' he purred, his finger quickening against her slick flesh.

His sensual commentary was turning her on even more. 'A-am I?'

'Mmm.' Suddenly his voice was urgent. 'And I want to be inside you.'

'So do I,' she whispered, dimly aware of him opening a condom—before he moved over her and she was angling her hips, eager for his thrust. But this time there was no pain, only heart-wrenching pleasure, and Emerald gasped as he filled her with his hardness.

Was that why he drove his lips down on hers? Were his bodyguards listening outside the door? she wondered wildly. But she was happy to be silenced by the sweetness of his kiss as he slowly moved inside her, and soon she was aware of nothing other than the sensual overload of her body as she gave into the most incredible orgasm of her life.

CHAPTER FIVE

DAWN WAS BREAKING when he woke and instantly Kostandin knew he was in an unfamiliar place. His eyelashes flickered open. The floor of the embassy's grandest salon, to be precise. Which was a first, he thought wryly.

Slowly, he acclimatised himself to the pale light which was filtering in through the unshuttered windows. The fire in the grate must have died some time ago, because the room was colder—a fact slammed home by the fact that they were both naked and lying on the floor, with Emerald snuggled up next to him, fast asleep. At least they were covered by a soft, cashmere throw—wrenching that from one of the nearby sofas had been the last thing he'd done before slipping into a blissful form of unconsciousness and having the best night's sleep in years.

He turned his head to look at her. The dark shadows under her eyes he'd noticed earlier must have been there for a reason because it seemed her need for sleep was as great as his—but then he guessed that sex like that took it out of you in more ways than one. Hell, yes. Despite the fierce hunger which had ambushed him, the first time had been slow and utterly...*perfect*—the second time even better. He stretched luxuriously. Her blonde hair was spread out over the rug like a gleaming cloth of pale gold satin. Her breathing was steady, her cheeks gently flushed, and her body...

Man, her body.

He felt another shaft of lust, his attention captivated by one rosy nipple peeping out from the blanket, and couldn't resist reaching out to glide his thumb over it, feeling the flesh grow pert beneath his questing fingers. As his groin began to thicken, he bent his head to flick his tongue against the puckered tip and heard her soft moan of appreciation.

'Oh,' she murmured, pouting a little in her sleep.

He grew even harder. But that was hardly surprising, was it? He'd been in a non-stop state of desire since she'd shimmied up to him in her waitress uniform, and since this was a limited window of opportunity, shouldn't he be making up for lost time? He pulled her close and as her tiny body melted into his, a deep sigh of satisfaction left his lips. He felt free. Deliciously free—and gloriously sated.

It hadn't been a false memory after all. Emerald Baker—as he had now discovered she was called—remained the best lover he'd ever had, as well as the most discreet. Was it that which filled him with an inexplicable desire to wake her up and tell her what was on his mind? To confide in her in a way in which it would be impossible to do with anyone else—even his closest advisors.

'Emerald, I'm thinking of abdicating in favour of my cousin. I want out of this life, for good.'

His pulse slammed. Even acknowledging the truth to himself made him feel as if he were engaged in an act of treason. Lately his discontent had become harder to ignore and he knew it was something he needed to address very soon. But not now. Not with temptation lying right next to him. Why waste time in speculation when he could be losing himself inside her again, before calling for a car to take her home?

Sliding his hand between her thighs, he ran a featherlight fingertip over her rapidly engorging bud. Still half asleep, she began to moan as he slid his finger up and down in slick and delicious rhythm—her trembling body so responsive that he sensed she was going to come very quickly.

'Kostandin,' she murmured, her fingers reaching out to knead his shoulders, her lips whispering against his in a breathless kiss. 'Please.'

He needed no further entreaty. Pausing only to grab a condom, he rolled on top of her and thrust deep inside her, his hardness filling her, and she gave a small moan as he began to move. His prediction of how close she was to orgasm had been uncannily accurate, because within what seemed like seconds her muscles began to clench around him. Her body arched like a taut bow before spasms of pleasure dragged her under and he could hold on no longer. Surrendering to the siren call of her warm flesh, he choked out his fulfilment as she sucked every drop of semen from his body and he'd never felt quite so empty and yet so completely full, all at the same time.

Lost in the sweet aftermath like never before, he tangled his fingers in the split silk of her hair, his breathing ragged as he attempted to drag oxygen into his starved lungs. But then her eyelashes fluttered open and Kostandin was momentarily taken aback, because her expression wasn't what he might have anticipated in that split second of emotional transparency which always occurred when a woman was soft and sated with pleasure.

All he could see was a sudden shadow clouding her features as she let her arms fall from where they'd been clutching his shoulders, to suddenly wriggle away from him. There was something in her face he didn't recognise, though he noticed the sudden goosebumping of her skin, as if she were nervous. But analysis was inevitably tedious, so he didn't enquire about the cause of what looked like discomfiture, just stared into the emerald fire of her eyes instead.

'That was fantastic,' he murmured, echoing the words she'd spoken to him so long ago.

'Yes,' she agreed, her voice low. 'It w-was.'

But she seemed *strained*, he thought—and light years away from the woman who had demonstrated her physical desire for him so enthusiastically just a few minutes earlier. Before his marriage, the only complaint expressed to him by lovers was that he didn't really *talk* to them. Was it conversation she was feeling deprived of? he wondered, as a sense of unexpected indulgence crept over him.

'You know, I wasn't really expecting to see you last night,' he said, with a lazy yawn. 'I thought you would have moved on by now. Yet there you were. Still working at the club. Still wearing that black and white uniform. It is sometimes comforting to realise how little in life changes,' he observed. 'Particularly when so much of my own has altered beyond recognition.'

'Yes.'

Her lashes had fluttered down to conceal her eyes and when she opened them again, he could see that same disquiet lurking in their green depths. Was it embarrassment? But if so, *why*?

She cleared her throat. 'Actually, I don't work there any more.'

He frowned. 'But—'

'I blagged myself an extra shift.'

His frown deepened as unease began to whisper over his skin. 'Because you knew I'd be there?'

A long pause followed and beneath the soft blanket, she shifted her weight a little.

'Yes.'

Kostandin's lips curved. Of course. No wonder she was looking embarrassed. It was a pretty bold thing to do. So did that mean she was stalking him, or should he take her impudence as a compliment? In the wake of such intense sexual satisfaction, how could it be anything other than the latter—and why not make the most of it?

'I'm flattered,' he murmured. 'More than flattered. In fact, it's a pity we aren't able to spend a little more time together, but I have to fly to Paris later this morning.' There was a pause. 'But there's no reason why we can't put something in the diary. I'm back in London at the end of the month. I'm sure we could fit in another meeting, just like this. If that's something which would appeal to you,' he added, his careless shrug morphing into another lazy smile.

But the delight he was expecting did not materialise, because she was shaking her head, like someone who'd been driving on autopilot and suddenly realised they'd taken the wrong road.

'Look… I should have told you sooner.' She swallowed. 'And there's no easy way to say this.'

'Don't worry, Emerald,' he replied acidly. 'I would be surprised if you refused, but it won't break my heart.'

She was biting her lip in a way which was making warning bells ring loudly inside his head when suddenly she sat up, all that hair streaming down over her shoulders, like liquid gold. She looked like a goddess, he thought achingly, when her next words drove every other thought from his head.

'You have a son, Kostandin.'

What she said didn't compute. In fact, she'd taken him so completely by surprise that Kostandin almost told her the truth. That he'd never had a child, nor wanted one. His determination never to procreate was his get-out-of-jail-free card. He felt the beat of a pulse at his temple. Because what good was a king without an heir?

'Wrong man, honey,' he drawled. 'You must be mixing me up with somebody else.' But then he noticed her expression. The trepidation which had shadowed her features. And the guilt. His eyes narrowed. Yes, definitely guilt.

Suddenly his heart was hammering with an emotion he didn't recognise as he sprang to his feet, pulling on his discarded trousers and turning his back on her as he zipped them up. It was a deliberately distancing movement—which also hid the betraying hardness of his body—so that when he turned to face her, it was with an element of his habitual, steely control. Because he must have misinterpreted what she'd said. Either that, or she was attempting to manipulate him. Mistake, he thought grimly. Big mistake.

'What the hell are you talking about?' he questioned coldly.

Emerald tried not to wince as she met his icy gaze, because he was looking at her as if she were a stranger—or an enemy—and she had only herself to blame. She had weakened her position by having sex with him, she realised. Why on earth had she done that, without telling him first?

Because you couldn't resist him.

You never could.

She forced the words out as succinctly as possible. It wasn't as if she'd never rehearsed them, was it? But having a conversation inside your own head was completely different from being naked on the floor of a posh embassy with a man looking down at you as if you had just crawled out from beneath a stone. With unsteady fingers she tugged the blanket further up her breasts, noting the reluctant flicker of his eyes as he followed the movement.

'You have a son,' she informed him and, instinctively, her voice softened. 'A five-year-old boy called Alek, who is the most gorgeous little—'

'That is *enough*!' His furious command cut her off mid-flow, before he lowered his voice into a deadly whisper. 'Do really imagine you can just walk into my life and start making unsubstantiated statements like that? Who the *hell* do you think you're dealing with, Emerald?'

She tried to stay calm even though his words had shredded through her maternal pride. He was shocked. Of course he was—and she must make allowances for that. She'd been pretty shocked herself when she'd stared at the positive lines of her pregnancy test and had sunk, trembling, to the floor. 'Obviously, it's not easy to get your head around the fact that you're a father—'

'Except that I am not. We had sex once, and I took great care to use protection,' he interrupted, before adding softly, 'I always do.'

Emerald bit her lip. If that last disclaimer had been made with the intention of hurting her by reminding him of how many women he must have had, then he had succeeded. Was it the sudden realisation of how vulnerable she was or his deliberate cruelty which made her want to fight fire with fire? Don't buckle under, she told herself fiercely. And don't let him patronise you.

'Actually, we had sex many more times than just *once*,' she informed him coolly. 'If you remember.'

But he didn't seem to be listening. His eyes had narrowed and he was nodding his head, like a man who had just worked out the answer to something which had been puzzling him.

'So last night was nothing but a set-up?'

She stared at him blankly. 'Excuse me?'

'You concocted an elaborate plan to get close to me—'

'It was hardly elaborate, Kostandin. I made one phone call.'

'Did you deliberately set out to seduce me?' he continued softly. 'Were you hoping I might receive your outrageous contention more sympathetically if we'd just had sex?'

Piercing pain stabbed at her heart. 'Please don't attempt to rewrite history,' she snapped back, all thoughts of staying calm forgotten. 'If there was any seduction—then it was mutual. I was hardly dancing in front of you naked, waving feathers, was I? You were the one who suggested coming here, who requested champagne. And you were the one who started talking about kissing.' She sucked in a deep breath. 'Anyway, none of that matters. The only thing which is important is what you're intending to do about Alek.'

'I don't actually have to *do* anything,' he informed her imperiously.

'No, of course you don't. And that is, of course, your prerogative,' she said, choosing that moment to stand up. But the deliberate dignity of her words felt at odds with the clumsy way she attempted to conceal her nudity, tugging on her modest underwear and grabbing her crumpled skirt and blouse. Wishing she were in a comfortable pair of sneakers—so she could run away?—she bent down to cram on Ruby's skyscraper shoes and when she'd fastened them, she straightened up and flicked back her hair.

'Okay.' She sucked in a breath. 'Let's forget we ever had this conversation. We can go back to how it was before. I've managed up until now as a single mother and

I can keep on managing. Nobody need know. Nobody at all. It won't bother me. I don't need you, Kostandin.' And then she shrugged, even though her shoulders felt as if someone had piled a ton of bricks on top of them, and she wondered if her deep sense of sadness was showing in her eyes. 'Because you're the one who's missing out, and for that I pity you. But at least you know,' she finished quietly as she picked up her handbag.

Still he didn't move, and then—almost as if he had remembered he was bare-chested—he reached for his shirt, his fingers slightly unsteady as he fumbled for the buttons. 'If this is true, then why tell me now? Why not before?'

'I can't believe you've even asked that question,' she breathed, not daring to tell him he'd missed a button-hole. 'When we...slept together, I knew it was never intended to be more than a single night. You made that very plain. And I was—' She wasn't going to come out and say she'd been happy about that, because obviously she had wanted to see him again. 'I accepted that,' she said. 'Soon afterwards, your brother was killed and I was sorry for your loss,' she added quickly as she saw his mouth harden. 'I would have written to you at the time, only it didn't seem... I don't know...' she shrugged '...appropriate.'

'Why? In case it looked as if you were using the be-reavement as an excuse to get in touch with me again? Plenty of women did.'

How hateful he could be, Emerald thought bitterly. But surely his attitude would make his rejection easier to bear. Much better for Alek not to have such an arrogant man in his life. Better for her, too.

'I discovered I was pregnant a couple of weeks later,' she said doggedly. 'But what with your approaching coronation and everything else that was going on, it didn't seem like the ideal time to approach you. I'm guessing that there never would have been an ideal time.'

She drew in a deep breath, trying to iron out the pain and the humiliation from her voice as she remembered how she'd felt when she'd discovered that everything he'd said about not wanting to settle down had been untrue. His assertion that he never intended to marry had been a big, fat lie. His subsequent fairy-tale wedding had been emblazoned everywhere and it had been like a progression of painful blows to her heart to see the darkly handsome groom looking down at his beautiful princess bride—a willowy stunner with hair as black as a sheet of shining ebony.

'And soon after that came the news that you were getting married,' she continued. 'Added to which, your new wife might have become pregnant at any time—so she would have borne you a legitimate heir. You certainly wouldn't have wanted one born out of wedlock.'

Had she been hoping for some shamefaced shrug of admission—some flicker of apology that he'd wed another woman so soon after sleeping with her? Because if so, he wasn't playing ball. Briefly his face tightened as if something she'd said had hurt him, but his eyes remained as cold as glass.

'But that was almost four months later,' he pointed out coolly. 'You had plenty of time to tell me before that.'

She bit her lip. He was right, of course, but she wasn't going to admit to the primeval instinct which had driven her behaviour during those early days. The terrible fear that such a powerful man might attempt to take control of her baby, or worse. Her heart thundered. 'Let's just say that I was very sick during the first trimester,' she said slowly. 'And I couldn't have stomached any kind of drama.'

Kostandin turned away from her. He was a master at controlling his emotions. At keeping them hidden from himself, as well as from other people. But for once it was proving hard not to betray his reaction and not just because Emerald Baker seemed capable of pressing all his buttons. She had ambushed him with this piece of information. Something with the potential to blow his plans for the future straight out of the water. He felt the twist of anger and regret. He didn't want to believe her. Every instinct he possessed was telling him it couldn't be so. Yet he couldn't just walk away, not until he had convinced himself she was lying.

'Take me to him. I want to see him,' he said, turning round to surprise the trembling of her kiss-darkened lips. 'Now,' he added harshly.

Her green eyes were startled. 'That won't be possible.'

'Why not?' he demanded. 'Are you afraid you're going to be caught out in a lie, Emerald? Perhaps I don't really have a son at all—maybe I'm just the richest and therefore the most useful of all your lovers.'

'You really think I would be that mercenary? Do you? Since when did you get so…*suspicious*, Kostandin?' Her lips folded in on themselves. 'Or were you always that way and I just somehow missed it?'

Pretty much, he thought bitterly. A deep distrust of other people's motives had settled on him from the moment he'd discovered that nothing was ever as it seemed. The royal world was one of smoke and mirrors and nobody ever told you the truth. They told you what they thought you wanted to hear. Or what they thought you should hear, in order to protect themselves.

It had been that slow drip-feed of subterfuge which had made him so cynical, though he had hidden that beneath a largely superficial exterior, once he had escaped from Sofnantis and the constraints of royal life. As a businessman he had been able to behave as he pleased. He'd worked hard and played hard, making himself a fortune and acquiring several beautiful homes in San Francisco, Paris and Kahala, in Hawaii. It wasn't until he had been dramatically recalled to the land of his birth to become King that he'd realised flippancy wasn't an appropriate trait for a monarch. It was about the only thing about his accession which had pleased him—the acknowledgement that he could retreat to his emotionally remote default setting and nobody would dare challenge him.

'Let's get a few things straight, shall we, Emerald?' he continued coldly. 'You engineered an opportunity to speak to me, but delayed your grand announcement until after you'd had sex with me. I can only conclude that was done with the intention of making me more… malleable—which is nothing but manipulation honed to a fine art. Yet now you say I can't see him. So why come here at all? What is it you want from me? Money?'

The distress which darkened her eyes was so intense that for a moment he found himself wishing he could retract his bald accusation.

'No, I don't want your damned money,' she explained. 'In fact, I'd like never to set eyes on you again. But this isn't about me. It's about Alek. I'm not stopping you from seeing him, but it isn't that easy and it can't happen at this precise moment.' Her verdant gaze swept towards the mullioned windows, where the pale sun was rising over the park. 'Mainly because I don't live in London. Not any more. My sister and I moved to somewhere much cheaper.'

'Where?' he shot out impatiently.

'Northumberland.'

His eyes narrowed. 'Near Newcastle?'

'You know it?'

'I'm not exactly a stranger to an atlas, Emerald,' he snapped. 'I know it's at the other end of the country, but that won't be a problem.' He glanced down at his watch. 'We'll just have to go by helicopter.'

CHAPTER SIX

EMERALD HAD NEVER been in a helicopter before and the sound of the whirring rotor blades was deafening.

Reaching inside her handbag, she pulled out her phone and met the hostile glitter of Kostandin's blue eyes. 'Can I get a signal here?' she yelled.

'Why?'

Perhaps he would like to confiscate her phone! 'I'd better let my sister know what's happening. I haven't even told her I'm flying in. Certainly not in one of these.' She gave a hollow laugh. 'Or that I'll be back much earlier than expected.'

'I'd rather you didn't speak to her,' he clipped out.

'Are you suddenly policing what I do or don't do?'

'Don't be ridiculous.'

Her eyes narrowed. 'Then why not?'

'Because forewarned is forearmed and I don't want the child gussied up in his Sunday best.' There was a pause. 'I want to see him as he really is.'

Emerald hesitated before dropping her phone back in her bag, trying to convince herself it was a fair point—though she was thinking more from Alek's point of view. He would have a fit if Ruby tried to smarten him up on a

Sunday morning at the end of the Easter holidays! And in a way, wouldn't it be better if Kostandin encountered him looking the way he usually did? With mud on his knees and his shirt half on and half off—and that infuriating little lock of black hair flopping over eyes, which were the exact same colour as his father's.

Better for whom? taunted a rogue voice inside her head. Are you secretly hoping the terse King will take one look at his scruffy son and decide to have nothing more to do with him?

'Tell me about him,' he said suddenly.

She should have been prepared for this, but somehow she wasn't—she was too busy imagining how Alek was going to react when Kostandin blazed into his life. The little boy was used to travelling on the bus, or in the beaten-up old car she shared with Ruby. Their idea of a treat was a film at the cinema and an occasional burger and chips. Wasn't there a danger he'd be dazzled by a shiny limousine and bodyguards and a level of wealth which was outside the realm of most mortals?

What had she *done*?

'He's…bright,' she said, dragging her mind back to the question. 'I mean, I know every mother thinks that about their child, but he really is. And he's doing well at school.'

'What's the name of the school?' he demanded.

'You won't have heard of it. It's the local village school, which has an excellent record,' she added defensively, because she certainly wasn't going to start apologising for Ambleton Infants'.

'So what exactly have you told him, Emerald? Does he even know who I am?'

'Of course not.'

'Of course not?' he echoed furiously.

She chewed on her lip. 'It was easier to be vague.'

'Easier for whom? You, almost certainly. You wanted to deny him his father, is that it?'

'No. Not at all. It's not that simple, Kostandin. And it's a bit rich for you to waltz in after all this time and start making judgements about how I've chosen to bring up my son.'

'Since I've only just discovered his existence, I wasn't in a position to do it before, was I?'

'No, you were too busy being married to a beautiful princess!'

'Careful, Emerald.' He gave a short laugh. 'You're starting to sound jealous.'

'I'm not jealous at all,' she lied. 'I'm just stating a fact! Anyway, I thought you didn't believe he was yours.'

'I'm keeping an open mind,' he said steadily.

And something about his quiet declaration took the wind right out of her sails. 'Do you really think I was going to just come out and tell him that his father is a king?' she appealed. 'Can't you see how difficult that would be for an ordinary little boy to understand? What if he started telling his friends in the playground and the teachers and other parents got to hear of it? People might wonder why the son of a monarch was living in a rented house while his mum runs a beach café, and come to the conclusion that he was telling porkies.'

'Porkies?'

'Pork pies. Lies,' she translated, reminding herself that the King of Sofnantis was unlikely to be familiar with Cockney rhyming slang.

'So what changed your mind?' he persisted softly. 'What made you come and find me?'

'I told you.' She licked her lips and tasted salt. 'You got divorced,' she explained baldly. 'And you were also in England, which made it easier to get hold of you...'

'There's something else. Something you're not telling me,' he filled in as her words tailed off. 'Am I right?'

Surprised and slightly impressed by his perception, Emerald expelled a reluctant sigh. 'Just lately, he's been asking me lots of questions about his dad. He's at that age. I didn't want to have to lie to him, but neither did I want...' She met the question which glittered from his sapphire eyes as the helicopter began to make its descent. 'I didn't want him to start fantasising, or hero-worshipping a powerful king who lived in a faraway land, and becoming dissatisfied with the life he's already got.'

Had she told him too much, by making him aware of her vulnerabilities and fears? Because surely that would increase his power over her. But although his expression grew flinty, his only remark as two SUVs with blacked-out windows drove towards them was to ask for her address.

'I'm driving,' he said abruptly as he slid behind the wheel and gestured for her to get in.

Emerald had never been driven by him before but as the car pulled away, it had the effect of making everything seem almost *normal*. If it weren't for the bodyguards following behind, they could have been just an ordinary man and woman heading out into the countryside on an early Sunday afternoon in April, with pale primroses studding the banks of the lanes, and pink and white blossom frothing the trees like foam on a milkshake.

Here, the sky always seemed so big and the air so clean and it had provided a safe haven for her when she'd arrived from London, very pregnant and very scared. She was proud of the café she and Ruby had opened, and the cakes and puddings they made, which were now being bought by some of the hotels in the vicinity. But Emerald could feel her heart thudding with apprehension as they drew closer to Ambleton. What would he think of the place she'd grown to call home? Would he be shocked at its modesty—at the much smaller parameters of her life compared to the dazzling magnitude of his?

'We're nearly there,' she said, as the lightening horizon indicated the nearness of the sea. 'We could stop here, if you like.'

Kostandin cut the engine, seeing nothing but a vast beach beyond the fringes of the sand dunes. 'Where is he?' he demanded, aware of the sudden powerful beat of his heart.

She glanced at her watch. 'Playing football down on the sand, most probably. One of us always takes him on Sundays.'

'*One* of us?' He shifted in his seat to look at her, his voice sharpening as a previously unconsidered scenario suddenly occurred to him. 'And who would that be?' he shot out.

As he met the indignation in her deep green gaze, he acknowledged how powerfully his body was responding to her. She had misled him and manipulated him, yet still he wanted her. How was that even possible when he was so angry and confused? Hadn't he despised his own father for his devotion to a woman who had run rings round him?

'Do you honestly think that I would have had sex with you last night if I were in a relationship with another man?' she demanded, her tiny hands clenching into tight fists on her lap.

Kostandin felt a powerful beat of satisfaction as he registered her furious denial, but he was in no mood to try to placate her. Why should he, when she had used her body like a delicious weapon? 'I have absolutely no idea,' he answered repressively. 'All I'm doing is trying to establish the facts.'

'Well, the facts are these! My sister Ruby helps me with Alek,' she informed him, her voice shaking with rage as she pulled a scarf from her voluminous handbag and wound it round her neck. 'She has done from the get-go. I don't know how I'd have managed otherwise.'

'You don't have parents?'

'No, I don't. Not any more. My mother died a few years ago, when Alek was still a baby.' She gave a short laugh. 'And since my father had never wanted anything to do with us, I was never part of what you might call a traditional nuclear family.'

Maybe that was one thing they did have in common, he thought grimly. 'Go on.'

'When I discovered I was pregnant, Ruby and I

moved out of London and came up here. It was much cheaper and we were lucky enough to be able to rent a little café on the beach. We live in a cottage in a village nearby. The café's open every day but someone else does the shift on a Sunday, which means we can always...'

'Always what?' he prompted, his voice unexpectedly softening.

'Oh, you know. It's good for Alek to get some undiluted attention from one or other of us,' she said briskly, lifting her hands to smooth down her hair. 'We're pretty busy the rest of the time. Less so in winter. Ruby does most of the books and I do most of the baking and we sell our wares to local restaurants and hotels. Look— why don't we get out?' She reached for her jacket. 'We could walk across the sand dunes so they won't see us coming.'

'And is that for my benefit?' he questioned slowly. 'Or his?'

'I'm...' There was a pause. 'I'm not sure really,' she admitted.

Kostandin nodded and got out of the car, unprepared for that little note of honesty in her voice as the fierce blast of cold air slashed across his cheeks. But he was even more unprepared for what he saw in the distance as he narrowed his eyes against the pale glare of the sun. A small boy, chasing a plastic ball, which kept being whipped away from him by the wind. Nearby was a woman with hair the same shade as Emerald's and she was laughing, until she looked up and saw them, and then suddenly she wasn't.

Did her body language alert the child to the presence

of his mother? Because at that moment the ball was forgotten and the boy came hurtling across the beach towards them, his features becoming more defined with every step he took. At last he skidded to a halt in front of them, his expression alive with interest, and as he glanced at his mother Kostandin could see that his eyes were as bright as jewels.

As sapphires.

Kostandin felt the sudden squeeze of his heart. He didn't need the verification of various gushing profiles which had been written about him over the years, which inevitably described the intense blueness of his gaze, to know who he was looking at. Because it was like staring into a mirror and seeing a younger version of himself.

My boy, he thought.

Now the squeeze of his heart became tighter and he couldn't work out the origin of the feelings which were sweeping through him, like the waves which were rising out at sea. He felt dizzy. Elated. Confused. Scared—and he was never scared. His lips hardened.

His son.

His.

But hot on the heels of all this uncommon emotion came the mental clanging of a door as he realised that the possibility of living like a commoner was now closed to him for ever. He was back in his gilded prison, only this time for good. The discovery of an heir had changed everything. *Everything.* His bloodline had been continued, without him knowing, and his succession was now secured. He turned his head to look at the woman who had trapped him by bearing a baby he had never asked for, but the breathless sound of a child's voice meant that she was distracted from his accusing stare.

'Mummy! Mummy!'

His heart still pounding, Kostandin watched as Emerald scooped him up and whirled him round and round. The little boy was squealing with unbridled excitement, but all the time he was aware of those identical eyes surveying him curiously over his mother's shoulder.

The woman with the blonde hair had now reached them and was also giving him the same silent scrutiny, though hers was markedly unfriendlier than the boy's. For a moment Kostandin was taken off-guard because the two women looked so alike. Uncannily so. Were they twins? he wondered as he stood and prepared for an introduction which instinct told him he should not attempt to initiate.

'Alek…' Emerald's voice was hesitant. 'I'd like you to meet Kostandin.'

'That's a funny name,' said the little boy as he slid down from his mother's arms and stared up at him.

Unexpectedly, Kostandin's mouth twitched. 'Yes,' he agreed solemnly. 'But it is a popular name in my country.'

'Where's that?'

'Sofnantis. Have you heard of it?'

A tousled black head was shaken. 'No.'

'It is a land far away from here where it is very warm and sunny.'

The boy shot a glance up at the leaden sky. 'Can we go there?'

'Alek!'

He could hear the slight desperation in Emerald's voice. 'Why don't we all go back home and we can offer K-Kostandin a cup of tea?' she said, her words stumbling over each other. 'Oh, and—I'm so sorry—I should have introduced my sister. This is Ruby.'

Kostandin extended his hand and after a moment the woman took it, though it was the shortest handshake he could ever remember. 'You're twins?' he questioned.

'Yes.'

'I had no idea that Emerald had an identical twin sister.' The rare smile he offered, which never failed to charm, was clearly failing him on this occasion.

The woman, who looked very much like Emerald, shrugged. 'I'm sure you didn't.' She gave him a long and steady look. 'Emmy said that the getting-to-know-you side of your...er...*relationship* was rather brief.'

'Let's go, shall we?' interjected Emerald hurriedly, the note of desperation in her voice even more pronounced.

And Kostandin knew he needed to take control of the situation. He could not allow the emotions of these two women to orchestrate events which would impact significantly on all their lives. It was for him to do what needed to be done, no matter what lengths he had to go to in order to achieve it. Again, he felt the punch of something unfamiliar as he looked down into startling blue eyes so like his own.

'You've left something behind,' he observed, and as the child followed the direction of his gaze they saw the plastic football being pulled precariously close to the waves.

'Race you!' said Kostandin with a long-forgotten spon-
taneity as he began to sprint towards the shore.

There was a split-second pause before the little boy
joined in and together they ran across the vast expanse
of sands. And although Kostandin had never lost a race
in his life, for once he was prepared to let it happen and
allow the little boy to surge ahead, with a jubilant shout.
And in that moment he felt curiously unfettered. The
air was clean and cold and fresh and the vast sky was
empty and practically nobody knew who or where he
was. How long had it been since that had happened? Not
since those days of heady freedom he'd been hopeful of
regaining and which Emerald Baker had destroyed with
her shock announcement.

But his brooding thoughts were interrupted by Alek
kicking the ball towards him, accompanied by a disturbingly recognisable grin, and Kostandin kicked it back.
An impromptu game of football followed until, eventually, they made their way back across the beach. The
two bodyguards had joined the blonde sisters and they
were all standing silhouetted against the dunes, watching them. A disparate group, Kostandin thought. Two
strands of his life suddenly blending into one. And he
didn't want it. He didn't want it at all.

He kept his gaze trained on Emerald. Beside her
smartly dressed sister she looked slightly scruffy and
anyone less like a queen would be hard to imagine. But
she would do, thought Kostandin grimly. She would
have to do.

'Is that your car?' asked Alek as they reached the
gleaming SUV and he handed the football to his aunt.

'Kind of. It belongs to my embassy.'

'What's an embassy?'

Kostandin shrugged. 'It's a little bit complicated to explain. How long have you got?'

Alek looked up at his mother and Kostandin knew he hadn't imagined the apprehension which made her soft body stiffen.

'Oh, loads of time!' declared the little boy, with a cheeky smile. 'Can I have a ride in your car?'

Kostandin smiled back. 'Of course you can. You can show me where you live,' he said softly. 'That's if it's okay with your mother?'

There was a heartbeat of a pause. 'Of course it is,' she said brightly.

Kostandin walked towards her, his senses firing into life as he grew tantalisingly close. He dipped his head close to her ear, so that nobody but she could hear.

'And after that—' he gritted the words out from between clenched teeth, trying not to be distracted by the tantalising drift of her scent '—you and I need to talk.'

CHAPTER SEVEN

'SIT DOWN,' HE INSTRUCTED, his rich voice harsh.

Emerald was still trying to get used to the sight of Kostandin standing in front of the unlit fire. The house was deathly quiet. Alek was asleep upstairs and Ruby had diplomatically gone out for the evening, leaving her alone with the King in the sitting room of their tiny rented cottage. Beneath her sweater, her skin was icy— her blood frozen by a mixture of emotions she felt too exhausted to analyse. It felt bizarre having him here, in her home, knowing his bodyguards were outside, their huge vehicles practically blocking the narrow lane. She tried to see the room as he must see it, but that only provided another heart-sink moment. She had tidied up as best she could but it was difficult to hide the signs that three people lived here and there wasn't really enough room for all of them.

Kostandin had offered—though he'd made it sound like yet another command—to take her out for dinner so they could talk, but Emerald had declined. The last thing she felt like doing was sitting opposite him and going through the motions of ordering a meal she felt too sick to eat. And where would they have gone? The local restaurant relied too heavily on its microwave and she hadn't wanted to dress up, even if she had anything remotely appropriate to wear. She didn't want him to think she was putting out for him, or trying to get him to seduce her. Which was why she was still wearing the same jeans and sweater she'd put on this morning when he'd driven her back to the London B&B to collect her stuff. She gave a heavy sigh. She was supposed to have spent the night in the cheap room she'd rented overnight—not sleeping with the King on the floor of an opulent embassy.

'I'd prefer to stand,' she told him stiffly. 'And since it's my house, shouldn't I be the one playing host, not you?'

His jaw tensed. 'You should have told me about the boy long before now,' he snapped and then his sapphire gaze narrowed. 'We're going to need a DNA test.'

'If you think I'm going to allow you to stab needles into the skin of an innocent five-year-old, then you are a very foolish man!'

'It doesn't have to be done like that,' he said, his voice growing exasperated. 'It can be a swab on the inside cheek, or a sample of hair—'

'And both are invasive procedures!' she howled, before remembering that Alek was sleeping upstairs and lowering her voice into a hiss. 'Which I wouldn't dream of subjecting him to. Apart from the physical intrusion involved, how would I even go about explaining why we wanted to do something like that to him?'

'Now who's being foolish? We're going to have to tell him *something*, aren't we? Unless you have a better idea.' His sapphire gaze bored into her. 'What did you think was going to happen when you sought me out to tell me I had a son?' he demanded. 'That I would just shrug my shoulders and say "good to know" and leave it at that? That I would walk away and forget all about it? I am a king, Emerald. I have my realm and dominions and palaces to my name. Any progeny of mine is in line to inherit all those things. Didn't you stop to consider that when you sought me out to tell me? Didn't you think that your actions would have consequences for him? For you?' His voice grew heavy. 'For all of us?'

His words were a shock to the system and Emerald found herself sinking down onto the two-seater sofa, afraid her legs might give way. Because the truth was that she *hadn't* given it much consideration. She hadn't been thinking about inheritance—she had just gone on a gut feeling that the time was right to tell the childless King that he had a son. The opportunity had been there and she had seized it.

But that wasn't the whole truth, was it? Hadn't she secretly wanted to see him again?

Of course she had.

She had experienced an almost visceral need to connect with the father of her child which wouldn't be quietened. She'd tried to convince herself it had nothing to do with her and everything to do with Alek, but now she wondered if she had been secretly scripting a foolish romantic dream, which had been further fuelled by the fact that he obviously still fancied her. Should she have stopped to listen to Ruby's advice instead of forging ahead with her plan?

'I'm sure we can work something out,' she prevaricated.

His blue gaze sliced through her. 'How?' he demanded. 'My country will not accept an heir to their kingdom on his mother's say-so. And please don't give me that wounded-puppy expression, Emerald. I'm just stating facts, no matter how unpalatable you might find them.'

'But he looks like you,' she whispered. 'You know he does. He's the spitting image of you. Anyone with two eyes in their head can see that.'

With a ragged sigh, Kostandin nodded, because her claim was irrefutable. Hadn't his empty heart missed a beat when he'd looked into those mirror-image eyes? 'Yes, he does. But Sofnantis is going to require more proof than an uncanny resemblance to its ruler. What if a whole legion of black-haired and blue-eyed boys made their way to the palace claiming I was their father?'

'Why, is that a possibility?' she questioned unsteadily. 'Just how many one-night stands have you had?'

He wondered how she would react if he told her that she had been the only woman who had ever made him behave so incautiously. But why give her the opportunity to misinterpret something which had been nothing more than an overwhelming hormonal rush, triggered by a pair of remarkable eyes coupled with sensational curves? 'My sexual history is nobody's business but my own. We're supposed to be talking about my son.'

'Make your mind up. I thought you didn't believe he was yours!'

He scowled. 'Your vehemence is nothing if not convincing and I could be prepared to accept that you are speaking the truth, if you were prepared to be reasonable.'

She stared at him suspiciously. 'And what would that involve?'

Kostandin felt the bitter curl of resentment. Up until this very morning he had seen the possibility of a new life—and now, in a single stroke delivered by this petite blonde, all his plans were slipping away from him. His eagerly anticipated freedom had crumbled into a hopeless dream. 'It isn't a question of what I want, but what I need. And I need an heir.' His mouth hardened. 'A legal heir.'

Giving her a few moments to mull over his words, he walked over to a far wall, on which hung a montage of black and white photos, all of them depicting Alek at various stages in his young life. There was an early shot as a newborn—scrawny with dark hair—morphing into a plump and smiling baby, a cute toddler and gradually becoming the little boy he had met today with the lock of hair flopping down over one eye. Kostandin's heart clenched and his voice grew husky. 'Did you take these?'

'Yes. It's a hobby of mine.'

'They're good,' he said, with surprise. 'They're very good.'

She blinked. 'Thank you.'

Abruptly, he turned away, not wanting her to see his expression, for he was damned sure she would try to use any softening on his part as ammunition against him. 'Without matrimony, this boy will have no official recognition and no legal status. He will just be seen as the

King's illegitimate son.' He paused. 'Some will even call him a bastard.'

'Don't—'

'Why waste time railing against an incontrovertible truth, Emerald?' he questioned, rigidly composing his features before turning back to face her. 'We have a problem which has a simple solution. In order for Alek to benefit from his royal parentage, you will have to become my wife.'

She leapt to her feet with a look of horror which should have been insulting but, bizarrely, it was no such thing. But then, she looked incredible in that moment in all her blazing defiance, Kostandin acknowledged— all life and fire and passion—and he felt the powerful beat of his heart.

'No!' she declared.

'No?' he echoed disbelievingly.

'I can't possibly marry you.'

'Why not?'

'Well, for a start you've only just got divorced!'

'What does that have to do with anything?'

'What will your people think of such indecent haste? Won't it make you look... I don't know...flaky?'

'Flaky?' He glared at her. Was there no limit to the insults she was prepared to let slip from her traitorous lips? 'My people will prefer the security of knowing their king is settled.'

'Well, what about Luljeta, then? How is she going to deal with it?' She sucked in her cheeks. 'No matter how "amicable" your divorce was, no woman is going to be happy to be replaced that quickly.'

Kostandin felt a pulse thudding at his temple and, as she dropped her gaze to the shabby rug, he found himself wondering if news of his surprise marriage had impacted badly on her at the time. He wondered how much to tell her because, despite his default setting of keeping people at an emotional distance, wouldn't the truth help facilitate what he wanted? Or at least, as much of the truth as he deemed necessary. 'Let me tell you something about my marriage.'

'Actually, I'd rather you didn't. I don't need a blow-by-blow account of what happened,' she put in quickly, unable to hide her instinctive flinch. 'I read the reports on the Web, just like everyone else.'

'Just hear me, will you?' he said impatiently and, although she looked displeased at his imperious demand, she went to sit on the window ledge, against a backdrop of snowy white petals from the blossom tree outside. And for a moment Kostandin was distracted. With the sunlight gilding her hair and her eyes as green as the burgeoning leaves, she looked utterly enchanting, he thought, before reminding himself of everything she had kept from him. He could not trust her.

But he needed her to marry him all the same.

'Luljeta was my late brother Visar's fiancée. The Princess of a neighbouring land who had been promised to him at birth. It was a territorial marriage,' he added bluntly. 'And her dowry was intended to bring a long-disputed piece of land back into the domain of Sofnantis.'

'Nice to see your country moving with the times,' she offered sarcastically.

'It is impossible to change centuries of history over-night!' he bit out. 'She was glad enough for the escape route offered to her, and the fact that it would enable her to get away from the influence of her father—a most malicious man.'

Her eyes narrowed. 'Okay.'

'The wedding preparations were in full swing when my brother was killed. He was reckless,' he admitted, unable to eradicate the disapproval from his voice. 'A risk-taker of the first magnitude. The ground was too wet, his horse too skittish and my brother was hungover. The hunt should never have taken place and the accident should never have happened. But it did.' He gave a heavy sigh. 'And his death put Luljeta in a difficult position—'

'Because your country wouldn't get the land if the wedding didn't go ahead?' she guessed. 'And that was something you weren't prepared to tolerate?'

'I didn't give a damn about the land,' he said, angry at her inference that he was motivated by greed. 'But I did care that my brother's fiancée would be subjected to unbelievable cruelty from her father if she returned to her own land, still a spinster.'

'Still a *spinster*?' she echoed faintly.

'I didn't write the language, Emerald,' he returned coolly. 'I'm just giving you a flavour of what it was like. Luljeta's father was known to be very sick, with only a few months left to live…which is why I offered to marry her in place of my brother. Except it transpired that he wasn't as sick as he'd led people to believe and took a long time to die.' He gave a short laugh. 'Which was why what was supposed to only be a brief marriage ended up lasting almost five years.'

'I guess that's what's known as a marriage of convenience,' she said slowly.

'Well, not really,' he answered acidly. 'It was never intended to be anything other than a marriage on paper. The fact that it overran was extremely *in*convenient.'

'But you adapted?'

He gave a wolfish smile. 'Human beings are by nature adaptable.'

She pursed her lips together, as if the implication behind this last statement was making her uncomfortable. 'And since you're offering me exactly the same thing, this kind of transactional relationship clearly suits your nature,' she added quickly.

'It isn't a question of suiting my nature,' he drawled. 'It goes with the territory. Royal families have been arranging marriages since the beginning of time. It's a safer bet than relying on the vagaries of emotion and so-called *love*. So what is your answer to be?' He narrowed his eyes. 'Will you be my wife?'

Emerald was glad she was sitting down, although the window ledge was hardly the most comfortable of seats. Kostandin had just asked her—Emerald Marigold Baker—to marry him. Not much of a proposal, it was true. No moonlight, or bended knee, or reaching into a little box to withdraw a twinkling diamond—which, in his case, would probably be the size of a small planet. Instead, he had clipped out a functional question and surely she should have clipped out an equally functional thanks-but-no-thanks reply, because what modern woman would agree to such a heartless arrangement with such a heartless man, even if he was the father of her child?

And yet…

She swallowed, forcing herself to acknowledge the thoughts which were buzzing in her head like wasps in a jam jar. There was definitely still *something* between them other than the son they shared. An unfathomable ease in his company for starters, which was bizarre when you considered their difference in status. And neither could she discount the fierce sexual chemistry which burned as strongly as it had ever done. The way he could make her melt inside with nothing more than a blazing gaze. The way he could make her laugh…

A cautious spear of optimism began to nudge at her heart. She'd seen the way Alek had interacted with Kostandin on the beach today. Afterwards they'd come back here and he'd proudly shown his father all his little football trophies. Even in the short time while Emerald had cooked Alek his evening meal, Emerald had heard father and son talking, sensing that a true compatibility could be possible, with her son having what she'd never had. A father. Wasn't it worth putting her fears of getting hurt on hold, for that one thing alone? As long as she kept it real. No more baseless dreams about love, or romance. This wasn't about love—he'd said that himself—it was about making a marriage work. That was the whole point of arranged marriages.

'Okay. In theory, I don't see why I shouldn't marry you,' she said cautiously, unable to hide the beginnings of a smile.

'Good,' he said abruptly, glancing at the watch gleaming at his wrist. 'In that case, we'd better agree a contract as soon as possible.'

Still in its infancy, her smile died. 'A contract?'

'Of course. I will have my lawyers draw something up, before you and Alek come to Sofnantis. It can all be done very quickly. I'd say a maximum of thirteen years together, until he is of age. A fixed-term marriage and then, if you are agreeable, we can dissolve the union.' He paused. 'Leaving you a very rich woman indeed.'

For a few seconds Emerald wondered if she might have misheard him, but the cool calculation on his face suggested otherwise. And how ironic that while she'd been urging herself not to entertain unrealistic dreams, her heart was now plummeting like a lift as she listened to the fine details of his proposal.

He doesn't care about you. You were never intended to be anything other than a one-night fling and now you're nothing but a means to an end. It's nothing but a cold-blooded business arrangement.

But maybe she should be grateful that his impersonal words were allowing her to see the situation clearly. Because she also had skin in this game and Kostandin needed to understand that. She glanced at the blossom outside, bright against the growing darkness. 'As I said, I agree in *theory*.' Her smile was tight. 'Obviously, there will need to be a trial period before I give you my final decision.'

'A trial period?' There was a moment of disbelieving silence. 'I'm not sure I get you.'

'What you're asking is huge, Kostandin.'

'Finding out you have a hidden heir is huge, Emerald.'

She met the ice of his gaze and tried not to let it intimidate her. 'Surely you don't think I'm going to yank Alek out of school and take him to a strange country, without having sussed it out for myself first?'

'Leaving him behind won't work. We have an international school in Plavezero which has an outstanding record, or I can arrange for him to be tutored at the palace.' His voice was emphatic. 'I want you to bring him.'

'I'm sure you do. But ultimately, this is my decision.' She saw his jaw tighten. 'What's the matter, Kostandin—are you used to always having the final say?'

'I'm a king—what do *you* think?' he snapped. 'Bring your sister along to help, if it makes you feel better.'

A flicker of apprehension whispered over her skin because the last thing Emerald wanted was her twin staying at the palace and giving her sometimes brutal advice. 'We have a business here in Ambleton, which can't just be abandoned,' she objected. 'What's going to happen if we're both away?'

'I can have people drafted in during your absence,' he clipped out. 'They can be here by the end of today.'

Emerald tried to imagine how the locals might react to palace staff taking the place of the sisters who ran the place in their own, slightly bohemian style. 'You think throwing money at everything is the answer?'

'It's certainly one of them, in my experience.'

'The answer is still no. Either I come on my own, or not at all.' She glanced at her watch. 'And now I think you'd better go—before Ruby gets back.'

In eyes as blue as cornflowers, she saw a flash of irritation which didn't disguise their underlying smoulder and, despite her inexperience, Emerald knew in that moment he was turned on by her. And the feeling was mutual, no matter how much she tried to deny it. A beat of heat thudded through her. Was Kostandin aware of her desire for him, or was she managing to successfully hide it? She wondered what would happen if he walked across that cramped sitting room and slid his hands around her waist. If he used all that potent sexuality to try to persuade her to his way of thinking, sweeping aside her objections and carrying her off to his land and insisting that Alek accompany them?

And didn't part of her wish he would? Wouldn't that absolve her of all responsibility, so that for once in her life she could let someone else make all the decisions?

But he did no such thing. The fire in his eyes had died and he was now regarding her with features so stony they might have been chiselled from granite.

'I had no idea you could be so stubborn, Emerald.'

'I'm a mother,' she said simply. 'And I will do anything I can to protect my child.'

She wondered what had made his face grow tense like that as he pulled the door open.

'I will be in touch tomorrow,' he said, stepping into the evening.

And then he was gone. Emerald could see torchlight and shadows as she closed the door behind him, but it wasn't until she heard his powerful vehicle reversing down the lane that she slumped down on the sofa, head in her hands.

And that was where Ruby found her.

'Well? What happened?' demanded her sister, looking around as if expecting their royal visitor to materialise out of thin air.

Emerald lifted her head. 'He's gone.'

'Yeah.' Ruby yanked the curtains shut and turned to face her twin sister, expelling a low whistle as she began to unbutton her coat. 'Seeing him in the flesh like that was quite something. I mean, nobody's going to deny he's sexy and powerful and it's easy to see why you did what you did, but you need a man like that in your life like a hole in the head, Emmy. He's got heartbreak written all over him.'

'I know that,' she said dully.

'So how did you leave it?' Ruby tipped her head to one side and a blonde cascade of hair so like Emerald's own shimmered over her shoulders. 'Did he offer money in exchange for a non-disclosure agreement? That's usually what happens in these cases, apparently.'

There was a pause while Emerald dragged her mind back to what had just taken place, but it seemed like a dream. 'He's asked me to marry him.'

Ruby gave a dry laugh. 'And obviously, you said no.'

'I told him I'd be prepared to go to Sofnantis to consider it.'

A long silence followed. 'You are kidding?'

Emerald shook her head. 'I was hoping you might look after Alek for me.'

'You know I will.' Ruby stared at her, askance. 'But why? Have you taken complete leave of your senses?'

Had she? 'Because I owe it to Alek. He needs to get to know his father.' Yet even as she said it, Emerald wondered if she was being honest with herself. Her feelings for Kostandin were complicated and part of her was curious to see if maybe they *could* make it work, as a couple. Would it shock Ruby if she admitted that? To confess that she wanted to break through that stony exterior to see if the man she'd once known still existed? 'How could I possibly explain to him, when he's older, that I wasn't even prepared to give it a try?'

Ruby shot her a sharply intuitive look—the kind which made having an identical twin such a double-edged sword. 'Just be careful, Emmy,' she advised tonelessly. 'That man is dangerous. He could threaten everything—all the happiness we've built together here.'

'You think I don't know that?'

But Emerald was discovering that danger itself was a very powerful aphrodisiac.

And wasn't that the most shameful thing of all?

CHAPTER EIGHT

'THE ROYAL JET has landed, Your Majesty.'

From behind his desk where he was fathoms deep in paperwork, Kostandin raised his head and met the gaze of his private secretary, who was hovering in the doorway of his vast magisterial office like an uninvited guest.

So. Emerald Baker was here.

A deep sense of satisfaction filled him. He hadn't seriously thought she might change her mind about coming but it had always been a possibility, and that in itself was bizarre. Their explosive sexual chemistry made him think of her as a sure-fire bet, but now he was being forced to recognise that the curvy blonde was no walkover. In fact, during their most recent interaction, hadn't her stubbornness been a match for his own? 'Well? Is there anything else, Lorenc?' he demanded impatiently. 'Can't you see I'm busy?'

'Indeed I can, Your Majesty.' Lorenc hesitated. 'I was wondering how you intended the press office to answer the inevitable questions which will arise once word of Miss Baker's visit gets out. A single woman,' he added delicately. 'And a commoner.'

Kostandin put his gold pen down on top of the pile of official documents he'd been signing and leaned back in his chair. 'This is the woman I intend to make my queen, but only you and my head of security are privy to that information for the time being. Are people already in place in…?' He frowned as he tried to remember the name of the village.

'Ambleton?' prompted Lorenc helpfully. 'Yes, Your Majesty. The boy is being well protected.'

'Good. So this is the deal. We keep Emerald's visit as low profile as possible, until such time as wedding plans are announced.'

Lorenc gave a nervous cough. 'In that case we really do need to have a statement prepared, Your Majesty. The biggest risk is the UK tabloid press who are always looking for a royal scoop. What if someone lets slip she's staying here?' He paused delicately. 'Wasn't there some suggestion that Miss Baker might not wish to marry you and if so, what then? It's a diplomatic nightmare, your majesty!'

Kostandin studied his aide through narrowed eyes and felt tension invade his body. He hadn't ever wanted a child—just like he'd never wanted to be King. His own childhood had been as miserable as hell and he had no desire to recreate a nuclear family of his own. But now the die had been cast and there wasn't a thing he could do about it. Did Lorenc really imagine that, having discovered the existence of a hidden heir, he would be prepared to let him be brought up in obscurity in England, with the possibility of other men in situ?

He was just about to reinforce this assertion when

he found himself recalling the tiny blonde's look of determination as she had faced up to him, insisting that this trip would be nothing but a probationary period. He had never had a woman oppose his wishes before— they usually went out of their way to accommodate him—but didn't instinct warn him that Emerald Baker might be as fierce as a tiger when it came to her son? What must it be like to have a mother who cared about you like that? he wondered, with an uncharacteristic wistfulness—which he quickly quashed so that he could glare at his aide.

'There will be no such statement,' he said bluntly. 'She might not know it yet, but Emerald Baker will be staying and she will certainly be marrying me. Do you really think any woman would ever turn me down?'

The aide gave a nervous smile. 'Of course not, Your Majesty. That was an extremely foolish suggestion on my part.'

'I couldn't have put it better myself,' Kostandin snapped. 'Have her brought to the Rose Room, will you?'

Lorenc bowed his way out, obviously keen to beat a hasty retreat when his employer was in such a testy mood, and Kostandin was aware that he had been particularly irritable since his return from Northumberland. His initial buoyancy at having persuaded Emerald to visit had been tainted by her decision to leave Alek behind. And yet part of him admired her protectiveness towards the boy, even if it had thwarted his plans.

Making his way towards the Rose Room, past servants who lowered their eyes as he approached, he felt as if the walls were closing in on him. Two sentries stood on guard, saluting as they opened the double doors, but Kostandin waved his hand in dismissal as one attempted to accompany him inside.

'No. Stay out here,' he instructed abruptly. 'I wish to be alone.'

But as the doors silently enclosed him in the famously rose-tinted chamber, it was sobering to acknowledge that he was never alone, not really. At any given moment of the day, the King's whereabouts were documented. Everybody watched him. Everybody listened to him. Rooms fell silent when he walked into them. In a crowded space, it was his company most craved by all. A few words from him were something to be cherished and dined out on—or relayed to grandchildren in reverential tones. For five years he had endured the strictures of ruling a kingdom and, just when had thought he was loosening the ties, the straitjacket was tightening around his chest once more.

Anger flooded through him. Why hadn't Emerald Baker told him about the child sooner? At least then he would have had time to accept the inevitable. Better never to have anticipated the sweet taste of freedom, than have it snatched away from him at the last minute.

Walking over to the French windows, he stared out at the tumble of early roses, liberated at last from the thick forest of thorns which Kostandin had inherited from his neglectful brother. The exquisite palace gardens which had provided a rare place of sanctuary in his father's troubled life had now been restored to their former beauty, and his heart clenched as he remembered the old man's pain and his suffering. He stared at a portrait of the late King which hung above the fireplace, an impressive row of medals gleaming on the jacket of his military uniform. But nothing could disguise the terrible sadness in his eyes—the acknowledgement of his physical courage waning beneath the infinitely more powerful shadow of his emotional weakness. And that was what 'love' did to you, Kostandin thought bitterly.

So deep was he in thought that he failed to hear the knock on the door. It was only when he heard a soft voice saying his name that he looked round and saw Emerald standing in front of him. And although he was prepared for the heavy throb of blood to his groin, he was surprised—and yes, irritated—by the accompanying thunder of his heart. Why was his response to her so intense that at moments it felt outside his control? He prided himself on restraint and the power of his will, yet with Emerald Baker he had broken every rule in the book. Having sex with her was the very definition of bliss—yet wasn't that kind of desire, at times, almost *debilitating*?

As his gaze flickered over her, he felt another beat of irritation. No other woman summoned before the King of Sofnantis would have dared dress in such a manner as this. Her honed arms were bare and through the flimsy material of her top he could just discern the faint curve of her breasts. She wore glittery sandals such as you might see on one of the cheaper market stalls in Plavezero and her hair was woven into a thick plait, which hung over her shoulder like a gleaming, golden rope. Against the exquisite rose-coloured mosaic of the ancient room, she cut an unbecoming figure. But she was beautiful. Very, very beautiful, he acknowledged hungrily as a pulse hammered at his temple. An angel in blue jeans.

'Hello, Kostandin,' she said.

Torn between desire and resentment, he forced himself to respond with the formality now engrained in him and perfected through the countless official visits he performed every year. 'Emerald. How delightful to see you.'

She looked at him cautiously. 'Do you really mean that?'

'Let's pretend I do. How was your journey?'

'Convoluted. And longer than it needed to be.' She glared at him. 'Why on earth did I have to fly to Frankfurt before getting on another plane? I would have thought you were rich enough to afford a direct flight.'

In spite of everything his lips flickered with amusement in response to her outrageous suggestion that he was being unnecessarily frugal. 'It made you more difficult to trace if you flew from Germany. It means the press would be unable to track your flight path. I'm trying to protect you, Emerald—and to protect our son—by keeping your identity as vague as possible.'

But she didn't appear to be in the least bit mollified by his explanation, just hooked her thumb into the belt tag of her jeans and continued to fix him with that faintly mutinous verdant stare.

'And I didn't realise I was going to receive such a rapturous welcome when eventually I touched down,' she continued.

Something in her tone alerted him to mischief and Kostandin frowned. 'Are you being sarcastic?'

'Why, is that not allowed?'

'It is not usual to insult the King in such a way,' he answered carefully, trying not to think about how much he wanted to kiss that stubborn little pout and have her sweet tongue thrusting inside his mouth. 'Especially not within the first five minutes of being in his company.'

'I hope that doesn't mean you're going to drag me off to the dungeons?'

'Please, don't tempt me.'

Tempting him was something she would like very much to do—no matter how unwise a prospect that might be—but Emerald put her bag down on a table which appeared to be encrusted with semi-precious jewels, determined to hang onto the bravado she'd been practising like mad on the way over. It had been an emotionally fraught journey. It was the first time she'd ever been parted from her little boy and she missed him. Added to that was her wariness about the future and what it held, which had contributed to the dry mouth and thudding heart which were currently making her feel so destabilised. But there was no point in coming here if she was going to be intimidated by Kostandin. She mustn't dwell on the possible pitfalls. She had to give it a chance. She had to give *him* a chance—for Alek's sake. And how could that work unless she spoke to him as normally as possible?

Yet nothing in her world seemed remotely normal any more. Her eyes had grown wide with wonder as she'd been driven from Plavezero airport, down roads lined with brightly flowering trees, to a predominately golden palace, situated close to a sparkling blue lake. Everything was huge and glitteringly appointed but it was the sight of the Sofnantian flag—coloured black and rose and green—which gave her the biggest ice-water shock of reality. Because Alek was heir to this incredible country, she thought dazedly as the enormity of what lay ahead really hit home.

She had to get it right.

She *had* to. She'd put so much into building a life for their son in Northumberland—so had Ruby, come to that—and she couldn't threaten that simple, happy existence unless she was certain that an alternative would be best for Alek.

Yet, so far, she wasn't at all convinced there could be any kind of future for them here. Jolted out of her comfort zone, she had felt somehow diminished from the moment she'd set foot inside the vast building, while Kostandin himself seemed to have grown in stature. She hadn't really known what to expect when she saw him again, though she'd thought of little else in the intervening days. She'd half wondered whether he might be clothed in some kingly concoction of military pomp or flowing robes, but that had been nothing but a stupid fantasy. Sofnantis was a highly developed market economy and its ruler reflected that in his choice of clothes. His immaculate grey suit could have graced any international setting but, despite its corporate overtones, it did zero to disguise the potent masculinity of the man who wore it. But then, Kostandin had once dominated global boardrooms, she remembered, before his sudden elevation to the throne.

With an effort she dragged her attention away from his sartorial elegance to meet the distracting glitter of his blue eyes. 'I thought you might have come to the airport to meet me,' she said, hating her voice for that give-away croak.

'Traditionally, the monarch does not make special visits to the airport to greet visitors, unless they are also royal, which you, most evidently, are not.' His gaze was cool. 'And please don't look at me that way, Emerald. All I'm doing is pointing out protocol.'

'You don't even make an exception for the woman you say you want to marry?'

'One prefers not to make exceptions to the rules. It avoids setting precedents.'

She had intended to stay calm but now frustration got the better of her. 'Is this how it's going to be between us from now on?' she questioned. 'Are you going to keep referring to yourself in the third person? 'One' this and 'one' that! When did you start talking like that?'

'When do you think?' he returned heatedly. 'When the weight of the crown was placed on my head and the sceptre in my hand. When I became King!'

'Well, we're supposed to be sizing one another up to see if we can bear to be married, not pulling rank,' she said. 'So if it's all the same with you, from now on I'd prefer if you treated me like a human being rather than one of your subjects.'

She saw the faint flash of incredulity in his eyes. Heard his quick intake of breath. It was a brief chink in his kingly armour and, in that moment, Emerald recognised that speaking the truth was the only way she was going to survive this.

'Very well. In that case, I shall attempt to be more informal.' There was a pause and suddenly his voice was a little uneven. 'How is Alek?'

Maternal pride rushed through her. 'He's okay. Ruby sent me some photos of him going off to school this morning and he looked happy enough.' She slid her hand towards the back pocket of her jeans. 'Would you like to see them?'

'Very well.' He inclined his head. 'If you wish.'

Don't knock yourself out with eagerness, she wanted to admonish—but fished out her phone and clicked onto the first image before passing it to him. 'Here we go. Look.'

He took the phone from her but his features remained shuttered and, try as she might, Emerald couldn't gauge his reaction as he scrolled through the photos. And wasn't the reality that she found his proximity so unsettling she could barely think straight? Was that because he had re-awoken her senses when he'd made passionate love to her on the floor of the embassy and the memory of that night was still too vivid for comfort? It made her want to touch him and kiss him—and everything else which went with it. But they hadn't even discussed what role sex would play while she was here, and it wasn't really the kind of subject you could just bring up in the cold light of day, was it? It might sound a little desperate if she said:

Kostandin, are you planning to sleep with me?

Was it going to become the elephant in the room? The thing they were both thinking about but which nobody dared mention. And wouldn't it be more sensible if they *didn't* have sex?

The bubble of her thoughts burst as he handed the phone back, the brush of his fingers like wildfire against her skin.

'I agree,' he said. 'He looks happy enough.'

Emerald felt a stab of disenchantment at his lukewarm assessment. Most people would have made a polite comment about Alek's general cuteness, even if they were only going through the motions. But Kostandin didn't have to do anything he didn't want to, she realised. He was an all-powerful king who was used to getting his own way and she should forget that at her own peril.

'He must get his sunny disposition from me,' she said airily, but his only response was to reach towards a previously unnoticed golden bell set into one of the richly panelled walls.

'I have work to do,' he said abruptly. 'I will ring for someone to take you to your rooms, and we can meet for dinner later.'

Unwilling to be dismissed so carelessly, she drew herself up to her full height. 'Or you could take me yourself?' she suggested boldly. 'To make up for your no-show at the airport.'

His expression was incredulous. 'You wish me to play the part of servant by accompanying you to your suite?'

She shrugged. 'Some people might call it being a good host.'

'Such a veiled criticism of the King is unheard of!'

'Even if it's true?' she returned.

Kostandin glowered at her, but his obvious irritation had no effect for she continued to look at him questioningly and, unwillingly, he felt a flicker of admiration. 'Oh, very well,' he conceded reluctantly. 'Come with me.'

He was acutely aware of being watched as he swept along the corridors with the diminutive blonde scurrying beside him, endeavouring to match his long-legged stride. As they headed towards the central staircase, there were lingering gazes from aides whose role was to be unobtrusive and servants who were supposed to melt into the background. But there was no such melting today. Their eyes were almost popping out of their heads and a hint of half-amused rebellion sparked inside him, because Emerald Baker was certainly not what they had been expecting.

Unlike Luljeta.

The thought slammed into his head. Luljeta had been the perfect Queen. Beautiful, high-born and expertly schooled in the art of being royal.

And yet…

Yet…

His footsteps slowed as he halted outside the largest of the palace guest rooms, hearing her soft inhalation of breath as he pushed open the door. Suddenly he found himself recalling the humbleness of her cottage and the personal touches which had made it seem almost *inviting*. The line of small football trophies above the mantelpiece. The black and white montage of a little boy with disobedient hair and blue eyes which were so disturbingly familiar. The remains of a home-made cake on the scratched surface of the table. Kostandin found his heart contracting with an emotion he didn't recognise as he watched Emerald taking in her surroundings.

'Oh, this is beautiful,' she said, and he wondered if she was referring to the many priceless artworks and antique furniture dotted throughout the roomy suite. But she was standing in front of the window and surveying the distant panorama of mountains beyond the lake, as if nothing gave her more contentment than the unspoilt beauty of nature.

But when he stopped to think about it, she was pretty unspoilt herself. There was certainly no artifice about her. No false lashes, nor bee-stung lips or hair which came courtesy of a bottle. Was that why he found her so intoxicating? Why he couldn't seem to tear his eyes away from the perfect symmetry of her tiny frame? The filmy shirt hinting at the strong body beneath. The faded jeans clinging to the delectable curve of her bottom, which the fall of shimmering hair almost touched. He found himself wishing they were naked on that four-poster bed, with him easing himself into her hot, tight heat—and his heart thundered in wild conjunction with the erotic path of his thoughts.

But her physical appeal had never been in any doubt, he recognised as she turned to survey him with those jewel-bright eyes. He should concentrate on the studied secrecy of which she was capable. He should remember that her baby bombshell had delivered the death blow to his dreams—her fecund body the means by which he was now trapped. And she had used that body again, hadn't she? With a calculation which had taken his breath away, she had waited until he was sated with the sweet aftermath of sex before telling him about his son. She had bided her time for a moment of weakness before delivering her *coup de grâce*. And that was the way women operated, he reminded himself grimly. Ruthlessly. Single-mindedly. Selfishly.

Hardening his heart against the soft beauty of her face, he pointed to a recessed golden button by the door. 'When you press this bell, a servant will appear.'

'You mean, like a genie from a lamp?'

'You can ask them for anything you desire, within reason,' he continued, refusing to rise to her flippancy. 'There is a library, a swimming pool and a cinema at your disposal. The grounds are extensive and a member of the horticultural team will show you around the gardens should you require. Dinner with be in the Silver Dining Room at precisely eight p.m. and formal dress is required.' He raised his brows. 'Anything you want to ask me?'

'Where's the Silver Dining Room?'

'Behind the gilded set of doors on that first wide corridor we walked down. But someone will show you.'

'I don't have any formal dress.'

He gave a click of exasperation. 'Why not?'

'Hmm. Let's have a think about that.' She tapped her forefinger against her nose in mock puzzlement. 'Could it be that most people might be a bit challenged if they had to dress up for dinner in an actual palace, with an actual king? Even my fashion-conscious sister agreed it was a big ask.'

He sighed. 'Then I guess you'd better improvise for tonight. But no jeans. Definitely no jeans. Got that?'

'Oh, yes, Your Majesty,' she replied gravely. 'I get it.'

He was about to turn away when something made him ask it, even though he'd been doing his best to push the thought to the back of his mind. Something which hurt his chest as he forced out the words. 'What have you told him?'

'Him?'

'Alek,' he growled.

'He knows I'm here for a week. He thinks I'm having a holiday in the sun—'

'No, not that,' he interrupted impatiently. 'What have you told him about me? Does he know I'm his father?'

'Well, no. Of course not.'

'Of *course* not?' he echoed furiously.

I thought it was too soon.' Long lashes shuttered her eyes into slivers of emerald and suddenly her expression was wary. 'And that something so momentous would be better coming from both of us.'

'So he hasn't guessed?'

'Kostandin, he's five years old. Do you really think he imagines that every new man he meets is his dad?'

A pause followed and Kostandin couldn't hold back the words which filled it, even though he knew they would hurt her. Or was it *because* he knew they would hurt her? Because he wanted to wound her as much as she had him, by guarding her news so secretively and destroying all his hopes and dreams? 'I have no idea, Emerald,' he answered stonily, 'just how many men he meets in the course of a week, or in what circumstances.'

Her cheeks became spiked with pink before her lips grew tight with fury. 'Are you…?' Her fingers splayed out over her throat, in an attempt to conceal the blotchiness which had suddenly bloomed there. 'Are you suggesting that I've introduced him to a constant stream of lovers?'

'Pass.' His eyes bored into her. 'Perhaps you'd care to enlighten me?'

Emerald curled her fingers into fists, feeling almost dizzy with anger and hurt. Not just because he was judging her, but because he was devaluing those two nights they'd shared by making out they could be two of many. That *he* could be one of many. Didn't he realise how special he'd made her feel, or was sex so mechanical for him that she had simply been another faceless woman in his bed? And if that weren't bad enough, all the time…*all the time*…he had been married to his beautiful queen. While Emerald had been slumped on the cold lino of the bathroom floor staring in disbelief at her positive pregnancy test, Kostandin had been enjoying sex with his hot new royal bride. How *dared* he take the moral high ground?

He was clearly waiting for an answer and pride was urging her to tell him she wasn't going to play to his one-sided rules. But pride had no place when measured against her son's welfare. It wasn't just her reputation she was defending, it was her lifestyle, too. In the last five years she'd lived a puritanical life and Alek had never witnessed her having an *overnighter*. How could he have done when every man who wasn't this man left her completely cold?

'You know I was a virgin when we met,' she said quietly.

'That's old news,' he answered. 'And not what we're talking about.'

'And since then, there has been nobody.' She bit her lip, because she felt almost ashamed to admit it. 'Except... except for you.'

There. It was out there. Her weakness. Her misplaced loyalty and, most of all, her vulnerability. She didn't *think* she'd told him in order to please him or get him to value her more highly, but maybe she was deluding herself. Because why else would a wave of disappointment wash over her as she watched the tight line of his lips become an ugly slash?

'Why should I believe you, Emerald?'

She stared at him. 'Why wouldn't you believe me?'

'Because women lie,' he said harshly. 'It's woven into their DNA.'

His harsh accusation took her breath away but even her righteous indignation did nothing to subdue her desire for him. Nor stop her from being achingly aware that a few feet away was the biggest bed she'd ever seen, hung with beautiful velvet drapes, embroidered with bees and birds and flowers.

Was he aware of it too? Did he realise that if he pulled her down on top of it and started tugging at her clothes, she would be lost? That in a tussle between mind and body she suspected her hungry body would win every time? Suddenly she knew she had to break the growing tension between them before she did or said something she might later regret.

'Do you know, I feel sorry for you,' she said witheringly.

'Sorry for me?' he repeated dangerously.

'For having such a desperately jaundiced view about women!' she snapped. 'So if you've got nothing else to say, maybe you'd better go, because I'd like to ring my son now.'

She saw his unmistakable irritation at being dismissed in such a cavalier fashion—and by a cheeky little commoner at that—but then the stony mask was back in place. The gleam of his eyes was cold, his mouth hard and unforgiving as he inclined his dark head with imperial hauteur and stalked from the room without another word.

CHAPTER NINE

YES, THIS BIT of corridor looked familiar. And so did that tall marble statue standing at the end. Which meant…

Sucking in a deep breath, Emerald pushed open the door and stepped inside, to be greeted by a diamond waterfall of chandeliers cascading from vaulted silver ceilings. But despite it being in the most beautiful dining room she'd ever seen—obviously—the only thing which truly captured her attention was Kostandin. He was standing by an open set of French doors, his features implacable as he turned to greet her.

'You're late,' he accused.

'Only ten minutes,' she said, trying to keep her voice calm—even though just the sight of him was making her heart slam against her ribcage. She was still brooding over the things he'd said earlier—implying that she was sexually licentious, or that she was *lying*. It seemed hurtful and unfair but it didn't seem to stop her gaze from drinking him in. His height was emphasised by the darkly formal suit and, in contrast, a snowy shirt provided a perfect backdrop for his glowing skin and glittering blue eyes. He was so gorgeous, she thought. And angry. Very, very angry. 'Sorry.'

'Sorry isn't good enough,' he iced out. 'You must realise that it's considered the height of bad manners to keep the monarch waiting.'

'And I keep telling you, Kostandin—I'm not your subject. I'm trying to treat you in the same way I would treat anyone else. Don't make such a big deal out of it. Anyway, I got lost. Big deal. It's a big place. Actually, it's massive. More like a maze.'

'It's a palace—of course it's big! What did you expect? Why didn't you ring for someone to show you to the dining room?'

'Because I wanted to find it for myself. You never learn properly if someone else always shows you the way. Anyway, I prefer to be independent. I've had to be,' she added pointedly, before shrugging. 'And besides, it's very inhibiting having servants around all the time.'

'Then you'll be pleased to hear we're eating in the garden. It's more private and low-key. I think you'll find it more relaxed out there.'

It was an unexpectedly thoughtful gesture and Emerald was touched as she saw that a table had been laid outside, sheltered by a bower of pale roses and resplendent with crisp white linen. Amid the gleam of silver and crystal stood tall, creamy candles, their flames barely moving in the stillness of the warm evening air. As she followed the King outside she couldn't help herself revelling in the heady atmosphere, because the intoxicating perfume of the roses made the scene seem intensely romantic. *And it isn't,* she reminded herself fiercely as they sat down beneath the faint outline of a curved moon, his next words confirming her thoughts.

'You weren't exaggerating when you said you had nothing formal to wear,' he observed, leaning back and subjecting her to a cool appraisal.

Emerald tried not to bristle. This was her best dress, one of those rarely worn pieces you could sometimes be lucky enough to pick up at a charity shop. Not the most cutting-edge outfit in the world, true, but it was serviceable, clean and a pretty shade of lemon—the exact colour of the primroses which bloomed in England every springtime.

Ruby had tried to get her to borrow some of *her* clothes but, once again, Emerald had resisted. She had wanted Kostandin to see the real her, but now she wondered if such openness had been an error. Maybe he was one of those shallow men her mother used to warn her about, who thought beauty was only skin-deep.

'Do you think you could manage not to be critical at least for the duration of the meal? I'm not in the mood for the sharp lash of your tongue.' She shot him a defiant look. 'Is that the real reason why you've brought me outside, because you're ashamed of people seeing me? Am I better hidden by starlight, rather than beneath the glare of those massive chandeliers?'

'Don't be absurd, Emerald,' he answered and, in the pause which followed, his voice took on a pensive note. 'If you must know, you look…lovely.'

Suddenly all her certainties were turned on their heads. 'I…do?'

'But living in a palace presents extraordinary demands,' he continued briskly, ignoring her need for reassurance. 'You need a new wardrobe and someone who will steer you in the right direction. Lorenc's assistant will be able to arrange for you to go shopping in Plavezero.'

'Whoa!' She put her goblet down, carefully avoiding the battalion of gleaming silver cutlery—she'd never seen so many knives and forks on one table. 'Not so fast. Why bother making any kind of investment until we know whether or not I'm staying?'

'Because you will need to attend official functions while you are here, to give you a flavour of royal life. Isn't that what we agreed?' In the fading light his gaze pierced into her. 'People will be watching and it won't go down well if you are dressed like...'

'Like what?'

'Why don't you stop feeding me opportunities to insult you, Emerald?' he drawled. 'It only creates conflict.'

'You strike me as the kind of man who thrives on conflict.'

'Or maybe you just bring out the worst in me,' he suggested softly.

Their gazes clashed in silent combat underpinned with something else. Something which was making Emerald's breasts grow heavy beneath her cotton dress and suddenly she hated her body's response to him and her failure to control it. Why was it this man—and only this man—who had the power to make her feel this way?

'So how is this all going to work?' she questioned thickly. 'Aren't people going to wonder who I am and why I'm here?'

'Of course—and inevitably, they will be asking questions. But I've been thinking about that, and about the photos you showed me.'

'What photos?' she repeated, her mind a total blank.

'Of Alek.'

Once again, it still felt weird to hear her son's name on his lips. *His* son, too, she reminded herself. 'The black and white montage?'

He nodded. 'You said it was a hobby.'

'It is. I take my camera everywhere. I like to snap portraits of people. When I have the time,' she added.

'Well, now you have the time.' His long fingers shifted restlessly as he picked up his water glass, as if something was making him uncomfortable. 'For a while now, my PR team have been urging me to update my image,' he confided reluctantly. 'According to recent polls, I am seen as stern and humourless and apparently it's not a good look. Perhaps you can help change the way people view me.'

'I'm not a miracle-worker, Kostandin.'

He smiled and it was like the warm sun breaking through a bank of heavy grey cloud. He often used to smile like that, she thought wistfully, wishing she could have captured it on film.

'Only Lorenc and my head of security know about your real status,' he continued. 'Giving you a purpose here will deflect any unwanted curiosity, even if it doesn't quite eradicate it. Of course, I will own all the copyright on the photos.' His eyes glittered. 'Just in case you thought they might be useful collateral which could be used against me at some point in the future.'

Emerald stared at him. 'What *is* it with you? Why do you have such a negative view of people's motives?'

He gave a cynical laugh. 'Spend some time in my shoes, then ask me the same question.'

Her response was stifled by the arrival of a fleet of servants, carrying delicate silver platters of food. Emerald helped herself to a spoonful of rice and smiled her thanks at the servant. She still knew practically nothing about Kostandin and, despite the fact that they shared a child, this was the first time they'd eaten a meal together. How crazy was that? 'You were the one who was just talking about questions being asked, so maybe I should ask you a few of my own.'

The barely noticeable raise of his forefinger was enough to make the attendant servants disappear into the indigo shadows of the garden.

'Please elaborate,' he instructed silkily.

'I'd like to know how…well, how you got to where you are today. Where you went to school. That kind of thing. A bit of your life story. You know.'

Kostandin frowned. He didn't know, as it happened, because he was out of practice. Nobody asked him personal questions any more. Even if anyone managed to penetrate his tight circle, unsolicited enquiries like this were strictly off-limits. It was another of the few favourable aspects of his position that it was a disadvantage to let anyone close. But despite his deep aversion to talking about himself, he recognised that for once he couldn't avoid it. He studied her heart-shaped face in the moonlight and felt the sudden hard beat of his heart. Because Emerald had a right to know.

'I was schooled here until the age of eleven,' he began matter-of-factly. 'After that I was sent away to board, in Switzerland.'

'With your brother?'

'No. My mother would never have countenanced that. She loved him far too much to ever let him leave.' He gave a cynical laugh. 'He continued with his schooling here.'

'And what was that like?'

He gazed at her blankly. 'It was an excellent school. I became fluent in French, German and English as well as—'

'No. That's not what I meant. I'm just thinking about what most people say when they go to boarding school. Didn't you miss your parents, and your brother?'

Kostandin resisted the desire to chastise her for interrupting him. If he wanted her, then it seemed he was going to have to put some work in.

And there was no doubt in his mind that he wanted her.

His gaze travelled over her. He had spoken the truth earlier—she really *was* lovely, despite her cheap dress and the absence of jewellery. But the golden cascade of her hair was adornment enough and he found himself yearning to run his fingers through those silken strands. He wanted to tiptoe his fingers up her bare thighs and feel the molten core of her desire. To slick his finger over her moist heat and make her buck and drench and call out his name.

But desire could make a man weak and, with an effort, he tempered it. 'No, I didn't miss my brother, for we were as different as mountains,' he said flatly. 'And neither did I miss my parents. I was glad to get away.'

'Oh?' She speared a slice of avocado. 'Why?'

'Why do you think?' he demanded. 'The relationship was…'

'Bad?' she questioned, into the silence which followed.

'Toxic.'

'Um…' she ventured. 'Were—?'

He waved his hand to silence her stumbled suggestions because wasn't this the perfect opportunity to spell out a few non-negotiable facts? To use the example of his parents as a warning of what she could—and never should—expect from him.

'My mother and father broke the mould of many of their royal contemporaries and married for love,' he bit out contemptuously. 'Consequently, the marriage was a disaster.'

'Because they were…incompatible?'

Her soft voice was tentative, and her interest seemed gentle rather than prying. As Kostandin stared into her green eyes he realised that, although her timing couldn't have been worse, he could never question her discretion.

'My mother was a very manipulative woman and my father fell completely under her spell. She used her beauty and her body to get what she wanted. You look shocked, Emerald,' he observed. 'Is it such a terrible taboo to criticise your own mother?'

'Well, it is a *bit* of a taboo,' she said carefully.

'Except that in this case it's justified,' he asserted, his voice growing harsh. 'She played him like a fish. She was openly unfaithful with a variety of different lovers and whenever he summoned up the guts to challenge her, she would just turn those great big eyes on him and tell him she loved him. And he would fall for that particular lie, every single time. And all because he was blinded by the foolish stars in his eyes.'

Emerald didn't rise to his bitter remark. She was used to listening to people and knew that if you remained silent it often encouraged them to talk. And Kostandin was on a roll now. The slick handmade suit and gleaming crested cufflinks seemed like a costume. The exquisite gardens and the lighted palace behind looked more like a stage-set than a real home. As if he had just been playing at the part of being King and suddenly the raw, flesh-and-blood man beneath had surfaced.

'A psychologist might cite my parents' example as the reason for my psychological distance with women, and they'd probably be right,' he continued softly. 'But that would only be a problem if either of us had unrealistic expectations.'

His gaze cut into her—a cold slash of blue with an edge of steel. 'And you and I are under no illusions about our feelings for one another, are we, Emerald?'

'Of course not,' she said.

Did he hear the uncertainty in her voice? Was that what made him feel the need to spell it out for her?

'I'm not looking for a *soulmate*,' he ground out. 'Not least because I don't believe such a thing exists.'

'Okay.'

'But on the plus side, I find your company entertaining.'

'Should I be flattered?'

'I think, if I were in your situation, then yes, most definitely, I would.' His eyes gleamed. 'And nobody could deny our sexual compatibility.'

'But you think I'm sexually compatible with all kinds of men, don't you?' she challenged. 'You implied that I'd had many other lovers. And although I was perfectly within my rights to have done just that, I didn't.' Her mouth tightened. 'I just don't like not being believed.'

He met her angry gaze and nodded. 'I did believe you,' he said roughly. 'I lashed out at you like that because I was angry, and I'm sorry. I believe too that Alek is my son and I will certainly not demand he undertake any form of DNA test.'

'Okay,' she said, slightly mollified by his unexpected apology.

'Listen to me, Emerald,' he continued slowly. 'We both want the best for our son, which is why I think this marriage could work. We could make it work. Just as long as you understand my limitations and accept me for the man I am.' His shadowed gaze gleamed out a warning. 'And don't ever make the mistake of falling in love with me.'

CHAPTER TEN

EMERALD WOKE UP in a bed the size of a football pitch when her phone began to buzz and she snatched it up, her heart racing when she saw it was an unknown number. What if one of the teachers from Alek's school was ringing, saying he'd fallen over in the playground and had been blue-lighted to the nearest hospital…? Until she remembered that England was two hours behind Sofnantis and her darling son would still be tucked up in his bed.

Pushing away the inherent fears which resided in the heart of every mother, she clicked onto the number. 'Hello?'

'It's me.'

Cursing her heart's racing response to a man whose dismissive words had sent her to bed in a stew last night, Emerald drew in a deep breath. 'Kostandin?' she clarified carelessly.

'You were expecting someone else?' he growled.

'You've never phoned me before. The number came up as caller unknown. Although I suppose it is quite useful to have it,' she added. 'Otherwise, how am I supposed to contact you in this great big barn of a place?'

There was a pause. 'My room is right next door to yours.'

'Is it really?' she questioned, her heart now demonstrating a rapid series of somersaults. 'I don't remember you mentioning that on the guided tour.'

'Maybe it slipped my mind.'

Did she imagine the lick of amusement which coated his deep voice? Was he *flirting* with her, she wondered, secure in the knowledge that he'd made her aware of his boundaries last night? She remembered the brittleness of his words as they cut through the warm air of that rose-scented garden. *'Don't ever make the mistake of falling in love with me.'* During the fitful night which had followed, she had fumed at his arrogance. And longed for his touch.

Yet her heart gone out to him, too—how could it not have done? Her own early life hadn't been easy as their hard-working mum had struggled to make ends meet. They hadn't exactly been reduced to boiling up potato skins to make soup, but Emerald and Ruby had experienced the very real feeling of never having quite enough of anything. Yet despite that constant financial insecurity, the twins had never doubted their mother's feelings for them—they had been loved and wanted.

Kostandin's growing-up sounded a nightmare in comparison, despite the lavishness of his surroundings. Two warring parents who made a mockery of their supposed love-match, and a mother who sounded as if she favoured his older brother and lied constantly to her husband. No wonder he had trust issues around women. She swallowed. No wonder he was so anti-love.

She cleared her throat. 'Was there any particular reason for this call, Kostandin?'

'One of Lorenc's assistants is going to take you shopping.' There was a muffled sound of him talking to someone else. 'She'll be there around ten. That should keep you occupied for most of the morning.'

'I'm not a dog,' she objected.

He laughed. 'Come to my office later, will you? I'm meeting a bunch of politicians at two. You can capture the occasion on film. But first, go and look outside your door.'

'Why?'

'Just do it, Emerald.'

Filled with curiosity, she cut the call and padded across the room, pulling open the door to see a white package sitting outside and she felt a kick of excitement as she brought it back into the room. The removal of waxy paper revealed a cardboard box and inside was a camera she recognised, because it happened to be the most expensive on the market—though never in a million years had she imagined she'd ever own one. She gazed at it, her heart racing like a train. The rudimentary handmade presents she got from Alek at Christmas and on her birthday she had kept and would treasure for ever, but she'd never been bought something so...

Stupid tears began to prick at her eyes. After a mutual agreement with her twin sister that they were a waste of money, nobody had bought her a present for years. She ran her finger over the strap. It wasn't the expense, it was the thoughtfulness—and she had never imagined that the sapphire-eyed King could be so thoughtful. Until she forced herself to look at it rationally and to remove unnecessary emotion from the equation. Taking photos was simply a way to disguise the true purpose of her visit to Sofnantis. How would it look if she pulled out her ancient and rather tatty camera and started aiming it at the mighty monarch? Kostandin's gift was merely a device to authenticate her supposed reason for being here.

But no amount of reasoning could dim her suddenly sunny mood and, after a scented downpour beneath the monsoon shower, she dressed and brushed her hair until it gleamed. Feeling a bit of a prima donna, she rang the bell and within seconds a freckle-faced maid called Hana was tapping on her door, offering a dizzying selection of breakfast options in various dining rooms within the palace. But daylight had an annoying habit of accentuating things you'd rather not see and the bright Sofnantian sunshine seemed to accentuate the shabbiness of Emerald's clothes. Did she really want to eat alone in a vast dining room, surrounded by nameless servants who might be questioning her appearance? No, she did not.

'Would it be all right to have my breakfast up here?' she questioned tentatively. 'I mean, I know it's not a hotel, but...'

'It will be my pleasure, mistress,' replied Hana. 'Your wish is my command.'

It was a weird sentence to hear in real life, but the maid's shy smile had the effect of making Emerald feel welcome and the breakfast which followed added to the elevation of her mood. A monstrous, white-cloth-covered trolley was wheeled into the suite and she tucked into creamy eggs and toast and a delicious bowl of lychees, realising she'd eaten very little the evening before. Her senses had been so achingly attuned to the formidable man sitting across the table that conventional hunger hadn't got a look-in.

She'd just put down the phone to Alek—'I'm *fine*, Mum!'—when there was another knock on the door, and she opened it to find a woman standing there, who, judging by her appearance, definitely wasn't here to remove the remains of her breakfast. She was tall and model-slim, her red hair as sleek as a creaseless green dress, which matched her elegant suede shoes. She carried a notebook and a pen and she looked at Emerald with an enquiring smile.

'Hi,' she said in a smooth American accent, which made her *sound* like a movie star as well as look like one. 'I'm Jessica Jones and I'm Lorenc's assistant.' She gave a faint frown. 'Did nobody tell you I was coming?'

'Yes, they did. The King explained I'd be going on a shopping trip. I just wasn't expecting...' Emerald's words trailed off because she could hardly come out and say she hadn't been expecting someone who was going to make her feel even more scruffy than she already did.

'Then...' Jessica gave her a questioning look. 'If you're ready—we could go?'

'Great.' Emerald grabbed her bag and tried to conceal it as much as possible as they made their way downstairs, where a brightly gleaming car was waiting in the sunshine. Climbing into an interior replete with silken cushions and bottles of iced water, Emerald wondered what exactly Jessica knew. Was her real status common knowledge among the staff?

'It's very good of you to accompany me,' she told the redhead as the car headed off down a tree-lined drive as wide as a river, towards an elaborate set of wrought-iron gates some way in the distance.

'My pleasure. I love clothes,' Jessica confided. 'And I have a degree in design from Harvard.'

'You're American?'

'Yup. I came to Sofnantis on holiday, fell in love with the place and was lucky enough to find a job here. Usually, I'm overseeing the interiors of all the palaces, so this is a real treat for me.' She looked Emerald up and down with an assessing gaze. 'So… I understand you need new everything and you need it, like, *yesterday*?'

Emerald nodded. 'Something like that.'

'Hmm. A highly unusual request, if I might say so. And super-intriguing, too. I mean, I used to accompany Queen Luljeta on shopping trips occasionally, but that was usually to see what the new season had to offer. I asked Lorenc to spill but…' Jessica twisted the grey pearl bracelet at her wrist and sighed '…that man is a closed book. So, why are you really here?'

The last thing Emerald wanted was to pretend to be something she wasn't, but telling the truth was bound to throw up a lot more questions and even if she *did* blurt it out, wasn't it slightly unbelievable—even to her?

I'm mother to the King's child and contemplating whether or not I should become his wife.

Jessica would probably look at her and wonder who the hell she thought she was. Anyway, she didn't have to *lie*, she just needed to be creative with the truth. 'Oh, I know the King from way back and he wants me to take a series of photos of him. Something to do with softening his image. And, as you can see, my current clothes don't exactly make me blend into the background.'

Jessica's brief nod acknowledged the evasion, but she smiled all the same. 'Then we'll just have to see what we can do about that, won't we? Like to see a bit of the city first?'

'I'd love to.'

They drove through the centre of Plavezero, with its creamy buildings, large green squares and complete absence of skyscrapers. It was a beautiful blend of the ancient and modern and Emerald soaked it all in, her gaze captured by a predominantly glass structure, its sharp edges softened by the judicious planting of flowering trees. Outside, a simple marble statue captured the image of a small girl, her head deep in a book. 'Oh, what a beautiful building,' she exclaimed softly. 'What is it?'

'The children's library,' answered Jessica, with a smile. 'Built by the King within the first two years of his reign, along with a new hospital and two new schools and countless other projects which have since been completed.'

'Wow.'

'Wow is just about right,' agreed Jessica. 'He's certainly very different from his brother. He came in and pretty much transformed the country, like a man on a mission. It's why the people love him, I guess—their stern and efficient king.'

There was a stack more questions on the tip of Emerald's tongue and perhaps it was a good thing their arrival at the store meant she couldn't ask them—because if she was seriously considering becoming Kostandin's wife, it wasn't terribly diplomatic to quiz the staff about her future husband, was it?

They were shown into a private room and offered tiny cups of strong coffee, while Jessica shot out a series of requests in fluent Sofnantian and various assistants reappeared, laden down with armfuls of clothes. There were skirts and trousers, dresses and jeans which were light years away from the pair she'd brought with her, and sets of brand-new lingerie which streamlined her curves in a way which was little short of miraculous. Dutifully, Emerald tried them all on. Some looked dreadful, some were too big or too long, but most were…

The full-length mirror reflected back a woman she didn't recognise—as if the old Emerald had been sidelined and replaced with shiny new version. And that was a weird sensation—as if the old her hadn't been good enough. But she went through the motions of gratitude all the same. 'Thanks, Jessica—though I'm not sure that these clothes are really *me*.' She glanced over her shoulder at the rear view of some pristine white trousers which would never normally have strayed near her radar. 'Does my bottom look huge in this?'

'Not a bit of it. The King said you were small but you're *tiny*.'

What else had the King said? Emerald wondered, her heart beginning to race. Was it that which made her blurt out a statement which was really a question she should never have asked? 'Queen Luljeta must have been fun to dress.'

'Oh, she was. She was *adorable*.' Jessica's voice

took on the tone of a serial dieter describing a choco-
late brownie. 'You know how some women can throw
on a piece of sackcloth and it looks like designer?'

'Well, not personally,' said Emerald, wondering, not
for the first time, why the marriage had imploded if
Luljeta was so perfect. Was *that* why Kostandin hadn't
touched her since she'd arrived here, because this palace reminded him of his ex-wife and her extraordinary
beauty? Even if the marriage was never intended to be
permanent, they must have known each other pretty
well during the five years that the union had lasted. An
unwelcome stab of jealousy poked at her heart and she
was glad of a distraction as Jessica pulled a final garment off the hanger and handed it to her with a flourish.

'Thought I'd go a little off-piste,' the redhead explained. 'This is something designed by one of our most
promising young fashion students who could do with
the exposure. Here. Try it.'

But Emerald shook her head as she studied the slippery piece of fabric. 'Oh, no, I don't think so,' she said
hurriedly.

'Why not?'

Because dresses like this were for women who
weren't like her. 'Because…'

'Go on. Just try it,' urged Jessica, her voice suddenly
growing kind. 'You know, you're a lot prettier than you
think you are.'

And even though she was probably only saying it
to be polite, Emerald found herself stepping into the
bias-cut gown and sliding her arms through the long
sleeves. Cream was a colour she wouldn't normally have

worn—close contact with small, muddy fingers would have made such a pristine choice impractical—yet to her surprise, it suited her. It was understated but it made her look sexy, she realised with a shock. It made her *feel* sexy, too—and she didn't want to feel that way. She didn't want to lust after a man who seemed to be keeping her at arm's length. And she didn't want to wear a dress which had obviously been designed for a woman as unlike her as it was possible to be. But despite her reservations, she allowed it to be added to the other purchases and, with an assurance that any necessary alterations would be completed by the end of the day, she was driven back to the palace.

She spent the rest of the morning trying to get her bearings in the royal residence. First, she explored a large section of the gardens and then she tackled the west wing of the palace complex where she found a large library, which contained a surprising number of detective novels. But all the time she kept thinking about the things she'd seen—the hospitals and the schools—and Jessica's remark about Kostandin being a man on a mission. She had implied that he was single-minded, and driven, and Emerald wondered if he would use that single-mindedness to convince her to marry him. Was she just another project? she wondered listlessly. Another goal to be achieved in his striving to be the perfect King and the antithesis of his brother?

Camera in hand, she was waiting close to the King's offices at the appointed time and her heart started racing as she heard his party in the distance. As Kostandin grew closer she could see he was surrounded by people—all men—yet somehow his towering height and darkly autocratic features made them appear as insubstantial as mountain mist. He looked deep in thought as he walked towards her and she wondered if it was the click of the shutter which alerted him to her presence, or the movement she made as she focussed her camera on a face which tensed the moment he spotted her, despite her best efforts to hide behind a tall, potted plant.

Their gazes met in one long and silent moment and instantly, she could feel herself reacting. A shimmer of awareness whispered over her skin and her nipples began to harden. For a split second she registered the smoky smoulder of his eyes but then the shutters came slamming down and, once again, he was all ice and steel.

The men were staring at her with open curiosity and as Kostandin drew to a halt they all followed suit. 'Gentlemen, this is Emerald Baker who is going to be taking a few informal shots of our meeting this afternoon,' he announced, slanting her a mocking look over the heads of the assembled group. 'No need to start sucking in your stomachs or your cheeks in order to look pretty. We aim to keep it real, don't we, Emerald?'

'Absolutely, Your Majesty,' she answered, wishing her face didn't feel so hot. 'Please. Just act like I'm not here.'

Easier said than done, thought Kostandin achingly as the petite blonde followed the delegation into his office and he sat down to begin the meeting. He had been the one to issue the invitation but now he was wondering why the hell he had granted her access to his inner sanctum like this when he was supposed to be working. Because she was distracting. More than distracting. Out of the corner of his eye he was aware of her moving around to capture him from different angles, and suddenly he was having difficulty concentrating.

He had been photographed ever since he could remember. Stiff, studied portraits taken on birthdays, or at Christmas, or—even worse—those dreadful 'informal' shots which were supposed to suggest that they were one big, happy family. These sessions he had tolerated without really thinking about them because they were part and parcel of being a royal, but never had he felt so exposed as he did beneath the lens being directed at him by the tiny blonde.

Last night he had taken her into his confidence and it appalled him now to recall how much he'd told her. Was it raking over the bitter memories of the past which had unsettled him, or discovering that he'd been her only lover—a fact which had filled him with a deeply primitive satisfaction? But he had deliberately fought against the powerful tug of his senses, sending her off to bed with a chilly warning about his emotional incapacity, only to spend the rest of the night lying awake thinking about her—an irritation for a man to whom uninterrupted sleep had always been a given.

He had woken this morning feeling distinctly out of sorts, with an ache at his groin which refused to be eased by the hardest of early morning horse-rides, or iciest of showers. The only consolation was that never had he felt quite so much in control. He had demonstrated—to them both—that he was capable of resisting her. And that gave him a perverse sense of pleasure.

'Do you have any thoughts on the matter, Your Majesty?'

Lorenc's polite intervention punctured his frustrated thoughts and Kostandin glanced up to find himself looking into the lens of her camera, feeling his body tense as he forced himself to contribute to the discussion. He was relieved when the politicians were eventually herded out of the office by his aide, who remained beside the open door, his expression bland.

'Would you like me to accompany Miss Baker back to her suite, Your Majesty?'

'Miss Baker will be staying,' Kostandin announced.

The faintest of frowns creased Lorenc's brow. 'You haven't forgotten your appointment with the Petrogorian King in fifteen minutes?'

'I'm hardly likely to do that when it's written on the piece of paper lying in front of me, am I?' Kostandin snapped. 'Just stop fussing and leave us, will you?'

Lorenc's obsequious head was lowered. 'Your Majesty.'

The door closed and suddenly he was alone with her, as he had longed to be throughout that interminable meeting. She stood on the opposite side of the room, her camera resting redundantly in her hands, and, despite the sophisticated new clothes, in many ways she looked almost demure. Sweet and simple—like a handful of daisies strewn over soft grass. Siren she most certainly was not, yet right now she was the most provocative woman Kostandin had ever seen. Surely the simple parting of her lips shouldn't be enough to make his groin ache like this, as if it were about to explode. And why was he finding it so difficult to stop thinking about licking his way over the luscious mounds of her breasts? Frustration flooded through him, but he offered nothing but a careless smile.

'Well?' he questioned. 'Did you get what you wanted?'

'I got loads of photos, if that's what you mean. Oh, and thank you very much for the camera, by the way. But...'

'But?' he shot out.

She hesitated. 'May I be frank?'

'Why change the habit of a lifetime?'

She gave a slow-motion shrug. 'If that session was supposed to be a charm offensive then I'm afraid it failed on just about every level.'

He narrowed his eyes. 'What's that supposed to mean?' he demanded.

'You said you wanted to dispel your stern image and then proceeded to scowl throughout the meeting. I don't think I got a single shot of you smiling. You just looked deadly serious the whole time.'

'The environment is a serious issue,' he ground out.

'Nobody's denying that, Kostandin.'

'Particularly when the minister in question seems unable to convince people in rural areas that rewilding the forests doesn't necessarily mean that wolves are going to be howling at their doors at every damned hour of the day,' he snapped.

'Yes, I understand all that. But you're still coming over as...' she shrugged her shoulders '...tight-lipped.'

'Tight-lipped?' he repeated dangerously.

'Well, yes.' She hesitated. 'You were before the meeting even started. You looked like you would rather be anywhere else but here.'

The irony of her words did not escape him and he gave a hollow laugh. 'Do you realise how deeply you insult me, Emerald?'

'That wasn't my intention. I'm just saying what I think. There's no point in me being here unless we're prepared to be honest with one another, is there? It's a difficult enough situation as it is, without me having to be polite to you just because of your position. What I'm trying to say is...' She looked at him with faint frustration. 'Well, I just don't remember you ever being like this before.' She hesitated. 'I mean, obviously I didn't know you that well—'

'Well enough,' he commented wryly.

A flush of colour rose in her cheeks as she acknowledged his words. 'But back then you seemed almost... carefree.'

Carefree? Was that really how she had seen him? Of course it was. It was how he had seen himself. He nodded. 'I was a different man back then.'

'So what happened to change you?' She put her camera down on the desk. 'To make you seem so...stern? Was it just the enormity of becoming King?'

His instinct was to clam up. To hide behind the veneer of royal privilege and berate her for insubordination. But maybe she was right. If their marriage was to be one of expedience, then why not at least be honest with her? If she was to become his wife, he must be able to tell her the truth, even if at times it might hurt her. Not just about his emotional coldness and all the things he didn't want from a relationship, but all the other things—which he did. And he needed their son more than anything, he reminded himself fiercely. Without Alek she would not be here.

And neither would he.

'What I am about to tell you must go no further.'

'This is completely off the record. For heaven's sake, surely I've proved that I'm not a gossip. Can't you just trust me, Kostandin?'

Her voice was soft and pleading but an instinct born of many years made him fight against it. 'I find it difficult to trust anyone,' he admitted gruffly.

'If you're hoping to persuade me to give up a life in England and come and live here with Alek, then you're going to have to try.'

'Is that an ultimatum, Emerald?'

'It's a fact.'

'Your insubordination is not appropriate,' he growled.

But she didn't appear in the least bit chastened by his admonishment, she just continued to stare at him with those curious green eyes. Abruptly, he stood up and went over to the window, staring at the tamed beauty of the rose garden and all that it symbolised. When he turned round she had perched on a velvet seat and, though he knew it was unreasonable for the mother of his child to ask permission to sit down, he still had to bite back his instinctive irritation that she hadn't done so. For all his complaints, how quickly he had adapted to the privileges of monarchy, he acknowledged wryly.

A ragged sigh left his lungs. 'When I became King, I discovered that things in Sofnantis were not as they seemed. The idyllic paradise was collapsing, because theft had been committed on a grand scale—'

'*Theft?*' she interrupted incredulously.

'Large-scale fraud by first my father and then my brother, who had used the country's reserves as their own personal bank account before bleeding them almost dry. My father in an attempt to win back the love of my faithless mother—and we all know how that turned out.' He gave a short laugh. 'And my brother because he was an addict.'

He waited for shock. For judgement. But her face remained implacable.

'What kind of addict?' she questioned softly.

'Gambling. Alcohol. Drugs.' He shrugged. 'Take your pick.'

She absorbed this in silence. 'And did he go into rehab?'

'No, Emerald. Rehab is for people who want to get better, not for people who want to get high.' His voice was bitter. 'By the time Visar died, the national debt was astronomical and Sofnantis was sinking into terminal decline. I used some of my own fortune to develop the lithium mines which have been our country's saviour, and I've been working non-stop for almost six years to undo all the damage inflicted. Perhaps that might explain why I acquired such a *stern* demeanour along the way.'

There was a pause while she considered his words. 'But surely you must let your guard down sometimes?'

He thought back to that night on the embassy floor, before she had shattered his world with her words—and a night six years before that. Both times had been the ultimate in erotic pleasure and both times it had felt as if she had torn away a layer of his skin, leaving him raw and vulnerable. And he'd wondered how it was possible to enjoy something yet fear it, all at the same time.

'Rarely,' he answered repressively. 'A good king needs to be strong. A figurehead of resilience and power.'

'That's a pretty punishing standard to live up to.'

'I don't deny it.'

'And don't forget…' her voice was gentle now '…that a good father mustn't be stern all the time, because that's quite scary for a child.'

It was something he'd never even considered and perhaps his answer might have bordered on the defensive had she not chosen that moment to lean back against the wall, so that a shaft of sunlight transmuted her hair into a stream of purest gold which melted away his uneasy thoughts.

'So, how do you relax?' she questioned.

It was such an alien concept that for a moment Kostandin struggled to come up with an answer. 'I ride,' he said eventually. 'We have a stable of fine thoroughbreds here at the palace.'

'Perhaps I could come and watch you some time?' She hesitated. 'You know. To take your photo. Searching for that elusive smile.'

Kostandin felt his body tense. She was doing it again. Staring at him with green eyes which had darkened like the night sky—provocation oozing from every pore of her tiny figure. Mocking him and teasing him and making him want to hold her. To rock that perfect little body beneath his. To feel her heat and possess her.

But that wasn't going to happen until the time was right. A time of *his* choosing—and only when she had agreed to marry him and his son was here at the palace. There was a price to be paid if she wanted sex with him again, and he would make her pay for it. She would learn that he would not be manipulated by her, nor swayed by her powerful sensual allure. To wait would be to test his resolve, and he *liked* to be tested. If nothing else, it reassured him that the steely control on which he had relied so heavily all his life remained intact.

But right now he could feel that control slipping away—like the tide being dragged out from the shore. The air was thick with desire. Her body was soft with promise, while his was hard with need. He could see a pulse flickering wildly beneath the blonde hair at her temple and, although temptation was licking at his skin, somehow he managed to refocus, and block it.

'Certainly you can come and watch me ride,' he agreed carelessly. 'I'll text you and let you know when I'll be there.'

She nodded and he found himself transfixed by that glorious cascade of hair, shimmering down over the generous swell of her breasts, and he flicked a glance down at the light which was flashing on his desk, knowing he needed to get her out of there before he changed his mind. 'And now, if there's nothing further, I really must get on.' His voice was deliberately impatient. 'My next appointment is due and I'm expecting the King of Petrogoria, a notoriously private man who I suspect wouldn't take kindly to the presence of a photographer, no matter how much I might vouch for her discretion.'

'Of course,' she said stiffly as she grabbed her camera and headed towards the door. 'I certainly didn't mean to outstay my welcome.'

'Emerald?' he questioned suddenly.

She stilled, like an animal caught in the target of a hunter's gun. 'What?'

'Will you speak to the boy?'

'Yes, of course. I'm going to phone him when he's finished school.'

'Tell him…' His words died away and, for once, Kostandin wasn't sure how to continue, for he did not know how to speak lovingly to a child.

He did not know how to speak lovingly to anyone.

'Say hello from me,' he finished gruffly.

CHAPTER ELEVEN

SHE COULD SEE him in the distance—dark and fast and fluid.

Emerald's breath caught in her throat as she stood in the shadows of the stables and watched the rider putting the horse through its paces. She supposed it was inevitable that he should be astride a gleaming black stallion which seemed bigger and more powerful than any horse she'd ever seen. The man's ebony hair was tinged red by the fire of the rising sun, close-fitting jodhpurs emphasised the long, muscular legs and his white shirt billowed in the whip of the wind. Sometimes, she acknowledged wryly, the reality of Kostandin really did surpass the fantasy.

Was that his intention? Was he deliberately allowing her close, but not *too* close? Allowing her to witness from a distance his power and magnetism as he went about his day in a way which few other mortals would ever experience. Or was he flagging up the reality of this life which would also be her life, if she became his queen? She'd watched him opening a paediatric hospital with—for her—the heartbreaking sight of him holding the small baby which had been thrust into his arms.

She'd attended lunches and dinners which sometimes she was allowed to photograph before sitting down to eat, while at others she would be told by Lorenc that there was a privacy issue. She was the woman on the edges of the room who nobody was quite sure how to treat.

Yet behind the fantasy figure of the King was a man whose brother had been an addict and his father a spend-thrift. A king who had married a beautiful young prin-cess to save her from the wrath of her cruel father. His whole life seemed to have been governed by malign forces outside his control. No wonder he was such an enigma. She remembered the expression on his face when he'd asked her to say hello to Alek the other day. The emptiness which had clouded the brilliance of his eyes, when he had seemed almost...*lost*.

She wondered what might have happened were it not for the arrival of the Petrogorian King, which had forced her to beat a hasty retreat. Would she have had the cour-age to reach out and comfort him, as she had been long-ing to do? But she hadn't seen him for the rest of the day, and she suspected that had been deliberate. He had sent a message via one of the servants that he was hav-ing a private dinner with the prime minister, so what could she do? She could hardly gate-crash a meal with the head of state!

The morning sun was high in the sky now, bathing the stable yard in a rich, red light. Already the air was soft and warm as she watched Kostandin negotiate a series of jumps and she was so lost in the visual beauty of his riding that she completely forgot to record it.

Did he notice her suddenly reach for her camera and notice the sunlight flashing on the lens? Was that why he slowed the horse into a canter, before easing it into a steady trot and making his way across the yard towards her? She raised the camera and started to shoot, grateful that her suddenly unsteady hands had something to hold onto. And for the first time in her very amateur photographic career, she became aware of the camera's ability to make voyeurism acceptable. It gave her licence to stare at him and keep staring and she wasn't going to deny the pleasure that gave her. She zoomed in on his face, so that only his strong, slashed features were in focus. The patrician nose and sensual lips. The chiselled cheekbones and hard curve of a shadowed jaw, framed by tendrils of damp, dark hair. He jumped to the ground, giving the horse a quick pat on the neck, before a groom appeared to lead the animal away.

'Emerald,' he observed softly. 'This is a surprise.'

'You told me you rode every morning and were supposed to text and let me know. Remember?' She gave an exaggerated sigh. 'But alas, there was no text to be seen. As it happens, I heard you walk past my room earlier.' She met his challenging gaze with one of her own. 'Footsteps can sound very loud along that echoey marble corridor.'

He frowned. 'But I was extremely quiet.'

'And I'm a very light sleeper.' Something made her want to explain why. Was it a need to illuminate something of her own past, so that he might understand her a little more? Or was she hoping it might ease the residual ache in her heart from seeing him hold someone else's baby and realising that, because of her, he had missed the chance of ever doing it with his own son? 'Alek was a very colicky baby. He used to wake up in the night and I was always listening out for him, so in the end it becomes a habit which is hard to break.'

There was a pause. His eyes were hooded. She was afraid he might turn away. Please don't turn away, she thought.

'Do you miss him?'

She nodded. 'Yes, I miss him. I miss him like mad. I'm used to him being there morning and night, and all day at weekends and holidays. It's weird being here and having to communicate by phone all the time.' A lump rose in her throat. 'We've never had to do that before.'

He absorbed this in silence, nodding his head so that little droplets of sweat shimmered in the glow of the early morning light. 'What was it like?' he questioned suddenly. 'Those early years?'

The flare of hope inside her grew stronger. He'd never asked anything like this before. It felt like a step forward and she knew her answer was as important as the question itself. 'Having a new baby is always difficult,' she said carefully.

'Are you saying that to spare my feelings, Emerald?' he questioned wryly.

'No. It's the truth. The adjustment is a massive shock for everyone. They even call it baby shock. But I was lucky because my mum was there, at least for the first couple of years. And then, just when she should have been enjoying her retirement and her grandson, she caught some awful pneumonia and died.'

Her voice became a little hoarse at the memory and she cleared her throat. 'At least, I still had Ruby and she was absolutely brilliant. Money was tight, but we managed.' In fact, the hardest bit had been the realisation that every time she looked at her growing child, she was going to be reminded of the man who had sired him. The man in the damp shirt who stood before her, his face tight with an emotion she couldn't work out.

'You should have come to me,' he said roughly.

'Even though you were married?'

'Yes, even though I was married.'

'I was afraid,' she admitted.

'Of me?' he verified incredulously.

'Of the situation I found myself in. You see, my mum got pregnant by a man who was married to someone else and he did everything he could to get her to…to…'

As the stumbled implication of her words became apparent, his face grew tight. 'And you think I would have done the same?' he demanded furiously. 'That I would have told you to get rid of our child?'

'I thought not. I prayed not, but I couldn't be sure. How could I? You're a very powerful man, Kostandin, and sometimes that kind of power is difficult for a person like me to comprehend.'

For a moment it seemed as if he might contest her assertion, but he didn't. And perhaps some of her confusion showed in her face because suddenly he reached out and brushed his fingers down her cheek.

'You should have come to me,' he repeated.

His words pierced at her heart, filling her with a sadness and regret as she thought about those wasted years.

All that time when he could have got to know Alek, and vice versa. Did he consider her selfish in keeping the two of them apart—as if she cared about nothing more than the need to protect her own heart? But as she met the sapphire blaze of his eyes, she saw no judgement there, just the unmistakable smouldering of desire. She froze—too scared to move or speak in case she broke the spell—wondering if her eyes were conveying how much she wanted him to touch her again. Please, she thought. Just kiss me.

And suddenly he was levering her back into the gloomy light of the stable, pushing her against a bale of straw where even the stab of a few stray strands sticking into her back wasn't enough to puncture her hunger for him. He stared at her for a long moment before bending his head to kiss her, with an intensity which took her breath away. Her eyelids fluttered to a close as his mouth pressed down on hers and the urgency of his kiss seemed to match her growing frustration. Her fingers splayed greedily over his damp shirt, untucking it from his jodhpurs and burrowing her hands underneath and he gave a moan as she encountered the slick, bare flesh. As she tweaked his nipple between finger and thumb, he groaned again—as if she had wounded him.

'Hell, Emerald.'

'Or heaven?' she parried softly.

She could feel the thunder of his heart as he pulled her closer, as if to imprint the hardness of his body against hers. His erection was large and proud against his close-fitting jodhpurs and she gave an instinctive gasp of delight as she felt its outline.

'Kostandin,' she breathed.

'Can you feel me? Can you feel what you do to me?'

'Hmm. Not sure,' she managed, her teasing words having exactly the right effect, because he circled his hips against her very deliberately.

'Now can you feel me?'

'Yes.' Her voice trembled. 'Oh, my God. Yes.'

With a triumphant laugh he started kissing her neck and as the stubble of his unshaven jaw grazed her skin, she wondered whether it might leave a mark and stupidly, she wanted that. He began to unbutton her shirt and warm air rushed over breasts which were straining against the satin and lace of her new bra.

'And what's this?' he murmured, his fingertip outlining the proud thrust of a nipple.

'Oh,' she moaned as he dipped his head and nipped the silk-covered tip with his teeth.

His hand moved towards her jeans and helpfully she sucked in her stomach to allow him to slide it inside, his palm making contact with her bare belly before inching towards her drenched core, which was screaming for his touch. And just when she thought he might actually drag her behind the hay bale, or at least propose a breathless assignation back inside the palace, he dragged his lips away from hers.

'No,' he said roughly, wrenching his hand out of the front of her jeans.

'No?' Her word was husky and confused as she looked at him blankly.

'We are not going to do this, Emerald. Not here and certainly not now.' Quickly, he regained his composure as he tucked his shirt back into his jodhpurs and slanted a stern look in her direction. 'The King of Sofnantis will not be caught *in flagrante* in the stable block with—'

'A common little cloakroom attendant?' she questioned furiously, buttoning her shirt back up with shaking fingers.

'With a woman who is not his wife!'

She sucked in an unsteady breath, trying not to think about aching flesh and how much she wanted him to carry on touching her. 'Is this your not very subtle attempt to manipulate me into marrying you, Kostandin? By making me so frustrated that I'll agree to anything?'

'I am simply stating facts,' he said coolly. 'You wouldn't need to be an expert in the ways of royal protocol to realise how inappropriate it would be if we were discovered by one of the grooms. Think about it. At the moment you have no real status here, Emerald. You're just an Englishwoman on some spurious mission to take my photos.'

'It's not spurious—it's real!' she declared. 'I'm very proud of the photos I've taken, if you must know—even if you look miserable in ninety per cent of them!'

As if to contradict her, he offered the briefest flicker of a smile. 'But if you were my wife-to-be, your position would change. It would confer on you instant respectability and status,' he continued softly. 'And then we could do what the hell we wanted.'

'This is nothing but manipulation!' she howled. 'I told you. I'm not agreeing to anything until I'm certain.'

'You're just enjoying the power of keeping me waiting for an answer, is that it?'

'It's not particularly enjoyable to find myself in this curious state of limbo,' she admitted. 'But perhaps it's a good thing to make you wait, Kostandin—since I don't imagine it's ever happened to you before.'

'And what exactly are you waiting for, Emerald?' he challenged softly.

'Isn't it obvious?' she challenged. 'Let's just say I'm information-gathering. I'm not making any decision about the future until I'm as sure as I can be that it's the right one.'

A flicker of what appeared to be grudging admiration lightened the sapphire depths of his eyes, but with Kostandin you could never be sure.

'I'm flying down to the southern peninsula this morning,' he said carelessly. 'I assume you're coming with me?'

'Lorenc said he wasn't sure if there was going to be room.'

He gave the ghost of a smile. 'Oh, there's room,' he said.

Despite the low-grade throb of frustration which still plagued her, the day which unfolded was more enjoyable than Emerald had anticipated, on so many levels—because for once Kostandin kept his aides and bodyguards at a distance. She wasn't going to deny the buzz it gave her to travel in the royal helicopter—particularly when it was being piloted by the King himself, his usual stern expression replaced by one of very sexy concentration.

Emerald watched the reaction of the crowds who surged forward when they touched down and it made her heart do weird and twisty things when she saw their reaction. Jessica had been right, she realised. They really *did* love him—in spite of his stern demeanour. He moved with such grace and elan that suddenly she found herself wishing Alek could be here, to witness his dad making old ladies swoon and young sea cadets swell with pride. Wouldn't he adore it? Of course he would. But any little boy was bound to be dazzled by this and that had the potential to be dangerous. She mustn't let the glittering veneer of royal life blind her to the reality of the substance beneath.

Back in the cockpit, he slanted her a sideways look. 'I think we'll have lunch at my summer residence,' he said, before pulling on the headphones.

'Are you showcasing your property portfolio in order to impress me?' she questioned mildly, and he glittered her a smile.

'Trust me, it's worth a look,' he promised softly.

It certainly was. Standing in expansive grounds of lush, beautifully maintained gardens, the gleaming white villa was situated at the very tip of the peninsula, in a sheltered bay which protected it from the coastal winds. Just before landing, Kostandin hovered the helicopter over the entire property so she could get a bird's eye view and from here she could see the silver glitter of a private beach, a vast aqua-tinted swimming pool, as well as two tennis courts set into the sprawling grounds.

Beneath the shade of a vine-covered canopy, the resident staff served lunch on the terrace and Emerald tucked into figs, local goat's cheese and delicious salads, washed down with half a glass of an award-winning

Sofnantian wine. When she'd finished, she leaned back in her chair and cast her gaze towards the sea, experiencing a moment of pure relaxation. 'I wish I'd brought my swimsuit with me.'

Kostandin didn't respond to the longing in her voice, cursing the erotic pictures which began to play out in his mind as he pictured her in a tiny bikini. He knew of a sheltered cove which would have provided complete privacy and where they could have swum naked. A curve of bay with deep, transparent waters and smooth rocks on which to dry out unobserved.

He used to come here as a teenager, during those unbearable months when there was no school. Eager to escape the tensions at the palace, he had spent long days here—always with a different girl in tow—engaging in long sessions of sex which now seemed anatomical and mechanical.

How he had changed, he thought wryly. It would have been beyond easy to take Emerald to one of those hidden places. To have stripped off their clothes and slipped into the sea—the water silky against their heated flesh as they joined together in the most fundamental way of all, knowing that with her it would be dynamite.

His throat tightened. But it wasn't going to happen. Abstinence felt like his only weapon in this strange battle which was waging between them. She might call it manipulation, but he preferred to think of it as a method of getting what he wanted, from a woman who was proving to be very stubborn.

'We need to head off back to the palace,' he drawled. 'I have some work I need to do before tonight's reception.'

* * *

As soon as they got back Emerald cooled off with a swim in the slightly underheated palace pool and afterwards phoned Alek. They talked about his day at school—one of the boys had broken his tooth in the playground and Aunty Ruby was making cupcakes for tea. But his next question was a curveball.

'How's that man, Mummy?' he asked. 'The King man?'

Emerald's fingers tightened around the phone. Had she naïvely thought her son might have forgotten the intriguing stranger who had burst into their lives one cold afternoon and whisked his mother away?

'He's…' Her sentence tailed away. No suitable answer sprang to mind. She knew what she could have said. That she was as confused as hell. That her feelings for Kostandin were deep and complex, yet she had no idea what he thought about her. Sometimes his gaze was stony and remote—while at other times he looked as if he would like to devour her. How could you tell a child that sometimes grown-ups played games with each other and you had no idea what the outcome might be? She swallowed.

'He's very well, thank you, darling. He's busy being a king, and kings have quite a lot of work to do.' She smoothed her fingers back through her hair, still damp after her swim. 'He has a big country to look after. Today, he flew me in his helicopter—'

'He *flew* you?'

She heard the unmistakable note of hero-worship.

Why hadn't she missed that bit out? 'And we went to his summer residence,' she said hastily. 'Which is lovely.'

'What's a summer residence?'

'It's a posh way of saying holiday house.'

'Is it by the seaside?'

'Yes, it is. I'll send you a picture.'

'And is he playing football?'

'Football?' Alek's random query puzzled her until she remembered him kicking a ball around on the beach with a man who looked exactly like him, the chill Northumbrian wind whipping through two heads of dark hair, in a scene so deceptively normal that now it seemed to mock her.

And suddenly, she found herself wishing they were back there, away from all this glamour and glitz. She found herself wishing that her son's father weren't a king with untold wealth and power at his fingertips and all the baggage which came with that. If he'd been an ordinary man, mightn't they have had a better chance at happiness? she wondered wistfully. Or was she in danger of rewriting history just to suit her own narrative?

'When are you coming home, Mummy?'

The simple question floored her. He sounded so young. So lost. Was it that which made another shimmer of fear whisper down Emerald's spine? Because she hadn't really stopped to think about the consequences of her solo trip to Sofnantis, had she? She'd thought that coming here alone would protect Alek from the King's powerful influence, but maybe she had been naïve. Because that influence wasn't going anywhere. She couldn't and shouldn't deny Kostandin access to his son.

She stared out of the window, at the gleaming lake, acknowledging all the potential repercussions which were waiting in the wings. Because if she *didn't* marry the King, she was going to have to spend long periods apart from her little boy. Alek would be proclaimed as the heir and learn to live as a prince, and his life in England would seem very dull in comparison. As his world filled with crowns and horses and unimaginable wealth, there was the possibility she could be permanently side-lined—an unimportant woman who lived her life in the shadows.

A lump rose in her throat. Could she really take that risk? Could she bear to settle for a life of snatched and unsatisfactory telephone conversations and seeing her son being whisked away in a luxury car as he joined his father for half-term?

She stared at the oil painting on the wall, barely registered the bucolic landscape of the Sofnantian countryside. Yet if she *did* marry Kostandin… If she accepted the cold-blooded terms of his thirteen-year marital contract, wouldn't that provide the most secure framework— for all of them?

'I'll be back at the end of the week, darling,' she told Alek slowly. 'Not very long now.'

As she ended the call, she thought about Kostandin's behaviour towards her. He had granted her limited access to his company—a few meagre crumbs here and there—enough to take the edge off her appetite but not to satisfy it. He had kissed her passionately in the stables and then pulled away. Why, when his desire had been glaringly apparent to them both? Was it because of his need to control and manipulate, or was Luljeta's shadowy presence too profound to allow any other woman a rightful place here? He'd never spoken of his former queen—she'd only heard Jessica's breathless admiration for her. Emerald swallowed. No wonder she felt so small and insignificant in comparison to the willowy ex-wife who had graced so many magazine covers. Yes, insignificant.

But she was never going to discover the truth or take their relationship on to the next step if she continued to let Kostandin dictate all the terms. Despite protesting that she wasn't one of his subjects, she had still allowed him to summon and dismiss her at will, hadn't she? What had happened to the woman who used to banter with him in her cloakroom booth, who could give as good as she got? Who had so willingly given him her innocence because she hadn't been able to contemplate the alternative.

She took the memory card from her camera and slotted it into her computer and the photos she had taken of him began to appear on the screen, one by one. Kostandin the ruler, walking down a corridor with his advisors, his face so stern and cold. Kostandin the horseman, astride his gleaming black stallion, all strength and grace. And Kostandin the man, walking among the adoring crowds, his face occasionally breaking into a rare smile which transformed those autocratic features into a face of heartbreaking beauty.

She turned off the computer, knowing that her future depended on whether she was content to be passive—or whether she was prepared to assert her own needs and stop acting like his tame lapdog. She had to ask herself what she really wanted.

Her heart missed a beat.

She wanted him.

Not as a king, but as a man.

And not at some cold-blooded time of *his* choosing.

She wandered over to the wardrobe, her gaze lingering on the creamy dress Jessica had encouraged her to accept. She had rejected it as unsuitable but suddenly she found herself looking at it with different eyes. Such a grown-up piece of clothing could be a game-changer, she realised, if only she had the courage to wear it. Tonight there was going to be an official reception and it was going to be a proper dress-up occasion.

Could she slither into this slippery piece of finery and walk into a crowded ballroom? *Should* she? Her heart began to pound. Because no way would she look insignificant in this.

CHAPTER TWELVE

KOSTANDIN WAS USED to being the centre of attention. His royal status made people stare at him, obviously, but he wasn't hypocritical enough to deny that his physical attributes inevitably commanded the gaze of others, especially women. But although social invisibility was something he often yearned for—he now found himself intensely irritated by it. Or rather, by her. The diminutive blonde who had just entered the ballroom—late, he noted sourly—a camera held insouciantly in one hand and a small sparkly bag in the other. He was even more irritated by the throng of dignitaries who were all staring at her, as if a golden star had just fallen to earth. Kostandin tensed. How dared she be late in his presence and…what in God's name was she wearing?

His heart thudded out a primitive thunder as his gaze drank her in and he suddenly realised that this wasn't an Emerald he was familiar with, but a sexy and sophisticated stranger. Yet her dress wasn't especially revealing, certainly not compared to some of the others on display tonight. It wasn't low-cut and the floor-length sweep, which allowed only the occasional peep of a satin shoe, was positively demure. But the pale material which clung to her generous curves made her body appear to have been dipped in cream and the hair cascading down her back shone like liquid gold. She dazzled. She glowed. She drew the eye inexorably and suddenly he was filled with a potent desire which was incompatible with being in such a public arena.

He raised his brows in silent command for her to approach, his irritation compounded when she did no such thing—just slanted him a sunny smile as she raised her camera and began to focus the lens on his rapidly tightening features. And since he had invited her to do exactly that, he could hardly accuse her of invading his privacy, could he? Deliberately, he turned away, his mouth hard with displeasure. Let her photograph his back and see if she found *that* interesting! If she wanted to capture an image of the face she claimed could be so stern and forbidding, then let her first come and seek his permission!

But no such permission was sought and he was forced to endure a conversation with a new and very earnest ambassador from Khayarzah, who could hardly believe his luck in having the King to himself. A princess from a nearby country rather boldly introduced herself, but Kostandin was curt in response to her suggestion that he might visit her palace soon, because he certainly wasn't interested in the assignation she was hinting at.

The evening dragged on predictably, with people hovering in his vicinity, eager to shake his hand. And still Emerald did not come—until eventually, he was forced to turn around to look for her, feeling as if he had lost some kind of silent combat by having to capitulate like this. His gaze sought her out like a heat-seeking missile, unprepared for the sudden jerk of his heart when he failed to locate her. Had she gone? he wondered incredulously. Had she actually left the reception before the monarch himself, and committed yet another glaring error of protocol?

Finally, he spotted a movement on the terrace outside—a pale cream shape outlined against the lushness of the flowers and foliage—and he was unprepared for the sudden clench of his heart as he turned to Lorenc, who was hovering nearby.

'Ensure that I am not disturbed,' he instructed curtly.

'Certainly, Your Majesty.'

He began to walk across the ballroom towards the French windows and as he stepped onto the terrace the powerful scent of flowers invaded his starved senses. She stood with her back to him, a series of pale curves, photographing the roses in the dying light of the sun, seemingly absorbed in her work.

Small groups of people were standing nearby, enjoying the sunset as they drank from goblets of champagne, and he wondered if his demeanour was especially forbidding because they quickly began to move back inside the ballroom once they saw him. And all at once he was alone with her. Well, as alone as two people could be with a couple of hundred others close by. His heart was hammering, his groin aching like a teenage boy's and he was filled with the sense of something he couldn't begin to understand.

'Emerald,' he said abruptly.

Slowly, she turned around, her eyes veiled by her long lashes. 'Good evening, Your Majesty.'

Her voice was tinged with a note he didn't recognise and his brain was too befuddled by her presence to work out what that might be. She dropped into a deep curtsey, which suddenly became an exquisite form of torture because it accentuated the faint wobble of her silk-covered breasts. Was that deliberate? he wondered savagely. Yet women had flaunted their bodies at him countless times in the past and it had never made him feel like *this*.

'Get up,' he said, his abrasive tone proving an ineffective antidote to his sudden overwhelming sense of powerlessness. 'What are you doing out here alone?'

Obediently, she rose to her feet, a look of caution on her face, as if correctly identifying the pugnacious tilt of his chin. But her steadfast air didn't waver. There was a new strength and determination in her gaze tonight, he thought, which only added to her glowing beauty.

'The light in the palace gardens is so exquisite that it seemed foolish not to capitalise on it,' she answered equably. 'I've got some amazing shots of the roses, with that statue in the background. Would you like to see them?'

'I don't want to look at your damned photos. Why didn't you come over to greet me when you arrived?'

'Because you were glaring at me.'

'Was I?'

'You know you were, Kostandin. In fact, you're glaring at me now.' In the fading light her huge eyes looked as dark as polished jade. 'I never seem able to please you, do I?'

For a moment he was tempted to articulate his frustration at being trapped in a situation he'd been so close to leaving—and since she was the unwitting cause, wasn't it reasonable to rage at her? But he could feel his anger draining away and with it, his resolve—vanquished by the creamy thrust of her breasts and gentle curve of her hips.

Why prolong the inevitable and, with it, all his aching frustration? Why ruin the evening with the bitter truth and risk driving her away? His throat tightened. Too many times he had turned away from the longing in her eyes in an attempt to contain the way she made him feel. Yet who was the supposed beneficiary of all this self-denial? he wondered bitterly. Nobody. Least of all him. Surely he had demonstrated to them both by now that he didn't actually *need* her.

'Did you choose to wear that dress tonight knowing that every man in the room would be staring at you?' he questioned.

Emerald registered the smoky glint of his eyes and recognised that something between them had changed. She'd known from the minute she'd walked into the ballroom and their gazes had clashed, the dark fire in his eyes making her feel so heated that she had been forced to seek refuge outside. But even the cool evening air was having little effect on her stinging nipples and she wondered if he had noticed.

Of course he had. Someone looking down from space could probably see their pebbled outline.

'There was only one man I wanted to stare at me,' she admitted softly.

His eyes flashed an unmistakable glint of satisfaction. 'Well, your wish has come true, because here I am.'

'Who said I was talking about you?' She hid a smile and relented when she saw his outraged expression. 'Of course it's you.'

There was a pause. 'Does that mean you're going to marry me?'

'That's a bit of a leap, Kostandin. I haven't decided. The jury's still out.'

'Is there anything I could do to hurry your decision along?'

'You could stop pushing me away.'

'I've already told you the reason why,' he grated.

'In which case, there's nothing more to be said, is there? We seem to be at a bit of an impasse.'

He stared at her with what looked like a mixture of impatience and incredulity until, at last, he gave a sigh of resignation. 'Okay, Emerald. You win.'

'I win? You're making it sound like some sort of battle.'

'Which it is. And while it's an undoubted turn-on to engage in this kind of verbal sparring, I suspect that any minute now one my aides is bound to come looking for me, telling me that a very important person craves my attention. And since I am loath to have this fascinating discussion interrupted, I suggest we continue it upstairs, where we will not be disturbed.'

Emerald felt her pulse skitter because, even though this was exactly why she had worn the slippery dress in the first place, suddenly she was nervous at having her bluff called. 'But…you're in the middle of an official reception. Surely you can't just leave?'

'I am the King,' he drawled. 'I can do anything I damned well please. And it is winding down now anyway. What would please me most right now would be to take you to bed and put us both out of our misery.'

'Misery?' she echoed indignantly.

'Frustration, then, if you prefer. Isn't that what you want, Emerald?'

Emerald ran her hands over her dress, feeling the softness of her hips beneath her clammy fingers. Not really. She wanted so much more than that. She wanted him to whisper sweet words of longing and then kiss her passionately on the sunset-flooded terrace. To pull her into his arms and crush her against his hard body. To seduce her into such a state of mindless desire that she would go with him, wherever he asked— not to imply in that almost conversational way that they should have sex again. If it seemed impersonal that was because it was, she reminded herself fiercely. This whole marriage proposal was little more than a business arrangement.

But refusal was an option she couldn't contemplate. She didn't want to play games or act proud. She wanted to hold him and kiss him. To show him with her body what she didn't dare express in words. A mother's instinct told her he would be a good father to their son, but she wanted to get to the bottom of why he was so remote and forbidding—and how could she do that if he kept pushing her away? For once he seemed so gloriously accessible and surely she would be mad to turn down an opportunity like this.

'Yes,' she said, as carelessly as she could. 'That's exactly what I want.'

Still he didn't touch her as they set off through the grounds. There were no linked hands or a tender arm around her shoulder, but somehow that only added to the tension mounting inside her as Emerald followed him through the darkening gardens, where the scented blooms made the setting seem even more romantic. But romance was nothing but an illusion, she reminded herself. This was all about sex—plain and simple—and it would just have to do for now.

As they entered through one of the gilded arches she wondered what the servants would make of it if they were seen together, or even worse—the rather terrifying Lorenc—but a series of secret passages and quieter stairways shielded them from view, until they found themselves on an upstairs corridor she recognised.

'Your place?' she questioned tentatively. 'Or mine.'

'Yours, I think,' he growled softly.

As he pushed open the door of her bedroom, Emerald felt another sting of disappointment. She'd been dying to see his kingly quarters—perhaps with a view to eying them up as a future marital boudoir—and couldn't help wondering why he didn't take her there. Was he thinking about Luljeta? Was he unwilling to use the same bed where he'd spent so many nights with his former queen? Theirs might have been a marriage of convenience, but that didn't mean they hadn't enjoyed passionate sex. Maybe he was afraid he might use the wrong name at the crucial moment.

'You look nervous,' he murmured, noticing her flinch.

'I am a bit,' she admitted. 'Aren't you?'

Kostandin shook his head, luxuriating in the heady pulse of anticipation as he took a step towards her. 'All I can feel is desire,' he husked.

'Can we turn the light off?'

'Why would I want to do that?' he queried softly. 'When you look so damned beautiful?'

For a wordless moment they stared at one another until suddenly, he could wait no longer. Hadn't he demonstrated more restraint than it was reasonable to expect? He had shown her that he was capable of icy control when the need should arise and she would do well to remember that. The lesson had been taught and now it was time for play.

But he couldn't hold back the groan which erupted from deep in his lungs as he started to kiss her. She tasted of honey and roses and trembling sexuality. He loved the way she shivered as he reacquainted himself with her petite frame, stroking her breasts with rapt preoccupation until she made a little moan of assent.

His palms cupping her buttocks, he brought her up hard against his pelvis and suddenly her hands were running frantically through his hair as she came at him with an enthusiasm which was as provocative as it was untutored. She was almost clumsily thrusting her hips against his and the frustration of having the barrier of their clothes between them was perversely delicious. With a low laugh he gently propelled her backwards, his hands guiding her until she was pressed against the wall, the firm surface allowing easier access for his questing fingers.

'Oh,' she moaned as he skimmed his hand over her belly.

'Are you going to let me rip your dress off?' he drawled. 'I've been fantasising about doing that all night.'

She opened her eyes and blinked, her earlier nervousness replaced by sass. 'No way. This is far too beautiful a garment. It would be an insult to the designer.'

'Correct me if I'm wrong, but he isn't actually in the room with us.'

'She,' she emphasised. 'The designer is a she.'

He laughed at this before his expression grew serious, his jaw tightening as he located the concealed fastening. Sliding the zip down, he slipped the gown from her body until she was standing before him in nothing but some extremely hot lingerie, her generous curves coated in satin and lace—and that was when he lost it.

'I want you, Emerald Baker,' he rasped hungrily, unclipping her bra with unsteady fingers so that her breasts came tumbling out into his waiting hands. 'You are so damned...irresistible.'

'Really?' She wriggled appreciatively beneath his touch. 'Yet you seem to find it quite easy to resist me.'

'Not easy at all.'

'So why do it?'

'It doesn't matter. Stop talking and undress me,' he commanded.

She was obviously a novice but her faltering movements pleased him, though he grew impatient when she took so long to remove the stiffened collar of his shirt, as well as all the other formal paraphernalia. Before long his clothes lay in careless disarray by their feet and all he wore was a pair of boxers, while she was barely covered by the scrap of lace at her thighs.

'If only you knew just how much I want you,' he groaned, peeling away her moist panties from the cluster of pale blonde hair which whorled so seductively at her groin.

'I think I can tell,' she offered shyly as she carefully removed his boxer shorts.

The rush of air to his heated skin added yet another layer of stimulation to his already overloaded senses and Kostandin, driven by a desire which she alone could rouse in him, picked her up and carried her into the bedroom to tumble her down onto the bed. He moved over her, her body warm beneath his, the soft rise and fall of her breasts only inches away. He stared deep into her eyes and suddenly all that teasing flirtation evaporated.

'What is it you do to me,' he questioned unsteadily, 'that makes me feel so damned primitive?'

She bit her lip and all at once she looked sweet. Uncertain. And that made him want her even more.

'The same that you do to me, I guess,' she whispered.

He felt the thunder of his heart. The hot rush of heat to his groin and he was grateful for the wild hunger which drove the nag of unfamiliar questions from his mind. Eager to lose himself in the infinitely less threatening domain of her body, he lowered his head to reacquaint himself with her skin. He drifted his mouth to her neck. To the damp path between her engorged breasts. To the faint softness of her belly. And then...

'Kostandin!'

Her cry was ecstatic as his dark head came to a rest between her thighs, his tongue delving into the silken folds and making her quiver, feeling in control once more as he orchestrated her pleasure until she was begging him for release. He feasted on her for as long as it took her flesh to convulse around his mouth and then, when he could bear no more, he moved on top of her. But as he encountered her warm flesh beneath his, her eyes opened—her beautiful, green eyes—and she was staring at him with an expression he didn't recognise. Was it trust, or was it tenderness which was making the sudden clench of his heart almost as distracting as the hard throb of hunger at his groin? And why the hell was he feeling so helpless?

'Emerald,' he said, sliding into her slick heat and hearing her murmur his name, like a prayer. She gasped with pleasure as he filled her and Kostandin realised that this was different. Different from every other time he'd ever had sex and why the hell was that? But it was good. Oh, yes... So. Damned. Good. He tried to make it last, even after she'd shuddered out her pleasure again and again, but suddenly he couldn't hold back any longer. As hot and as hard as he had ever been, the spill of his seed shattering—the cry torn from his lips, incomprehensible.

Half dazed, he felt her hand slide around his waist, her fingers resting comfortably on the jut of his hips as if they were perfectly at home there and all at once he felt...

What was it?

Safe?

As if he'd wandered into a place where he'd never been before and was being given the opportunity to stay there, if he wanted?

His eyes snapped open as he chased the elusive thought before it disappeared, and perhaps he conveyed something of his disorientation. Was that why she snuggled even closer, until he wasn't quite sure where her skin began and his ended and instead of being two, they were one? It felt as close as when he'd been having sex with her only he was no longer inside her. So what was going on? Suddenly the feeling of safety—if that was what it was—felt claustrophobic.

Choking him.

Trapping him. Just as she had trapped him once before.

'Kostandin,' she murmured again.

But as he heard the emotion in her voice, he lay perfectly still, regulating his breathing until it was deep and even. Until her hand slipped away. And although

he heard her sigh, he steeled his heart against that wist-
ful sound.

Because whatever it was she wanted to say right now,
he didn't want to hear it.

CHAPTER THIRTEEN

IN THE MORNING, he was gone.

As she lay amid the rumpled sheets, her body aching with remembered pleasure, Emerald should have been prepared for the clench of disappointment, but somehow she wasn't prepared at all. Still half asleep, she sat up and looked around, as if searching for proof that Kostandin had actually been there, but the only sign of last night's passion was a pair of crumpled cream panties, lying discarded on the bedroom floor. The ultimate flag of surrender, she thought, slumping back against the pillows and staring at an oil painting of a man on a horse, positioned right opposite the bed.

Their lovemaking had been sensational. No surprises there. He had taken her to the stars and back. That feeling of being in his arms again had made her lose every one of her inhibitions. It had felt different. *Special.* As if it had been about more than just physical satisfaction. Or maybe that was just wishful thinking on her part. Was that the reason why she had started whispering his name afterwards—with several soppy words of affection close to slipping from her lips as she'd snuggled up beside him? But either he'd been asleep or been feigning sleep because she'd never got the chance to say them—and maybe that was best.

So now what?

The knock on the door had her tugging on a robe and running into the salon, unable to wipe the smile from her lips—though when she stopped to think about it afterwards, why on earth would the King bother to *knock*? Because it was Hana who stood there, the servant politely wondering whether she would like breakfast served in her room, since the hour was so late.

Emerald glanced up at the ornate face of the clock. How could she have lain undisturbed until almost eleven o'clock?

You know how.

It had been the best night's sleep she'd had in ages. Well, pretty much ever, really. While they'd been making love, all the questions and the tension had just seeped away and everything in her world had felt exactly as it should do. Okay, so the intimate pillow talk she'd been hoping for hadn't materialised—but maybe she should be empowered by what had happened, rather than wondering why he hadn't bothered to say goodbye this morning. Maybe he hadn't wanted to disturb her. Wasn't that what men always said in films?

You looked so beautiful I didn't want to wake you.

Shouldn't she build on all the good bits, going forward, rather than focussing on the negative?

'No, thanks, Hana, I'll come downstairs,' she said before cautiously testing the ground as a potential wife with a domestic enquiry. 'I suppose the King will have already eaten?'

Hana looked startled. 'The King never eats breakfast.'

Emerald frowned and not just because the maid's answer made her feel a bit stupid. Now certainly wasn't the time to fanfare the nutritional benefits of starting the day with a proper meal and setting a good example to Alek in future. Actually, today might be the day when they did a joint video call with her son... *Their* son. She felt a warm flicker of anticipation. Maybe Kostandin could do a virtual tour of the palace stables and introduce him to all his horses—what a thrill that would be for the little boy back in Northumberland.

She showered and dressed with extra care, determined to look the part as she pulled on a floaty lemon dress and a pair of espadrilles, before setting off downstairs. En route to breakfast, she decided to make a spontaneous detour. She would call in and say hello to her lover, because wasn't that the sort of thing a future queen was allowed to do?

In the King's outer office she found Lorenc, working industriously at his desk, and though the aide was nothing but courteous as he rose to greet her, his face wasn't exactly what you'd call *friendly*.

'Good morning, Miss Baker. How can I help you.'

'Good morning, Lorenc.' She smiled at him. 'I wondered if I could have a quick word with Kostandin? I'm wondering what's in his diary for today and whether there will be any good, er...photo opportunities.'

I'm afraid that won't be possible.'

Something about his tone made the smile freeze on her lips. 'Oh? Why not?'

'The King has already left for a meeting at the Sof-nantian parliament.'

Don't ask it.

Definitely don't ask it.

She asked it. 'Did he…did he leave a message for me?'

Lorenc's eyes narrowed and she wondered if he looked almost *regretful*. 'I am afraid not. He really is exceptionally busy today, Miss Baker,' he informed her smoothly, walking towards the door before holding it open for her. 'But I will certainly tell him you were looking for him.'

She didn't know what made her peer across to the opposite side of the office—only that her heart started slamming when she saw the portrait lying on top of a large, unoccupied desk. An oil painting of a woman whose face she knew so well, even though they'd never met. A woman with a fall of jet-dark hair and eyes the colour of bright amber. Luljeta.

She opened her lips to demand to know what it was doing there, before shutting them and wondering if she'd taken complete leave of her senses. Why abandon her dignity by displaying jealousy and risk being regarded with pity, or scorn? She doubted Kostandin's fiercely loyal aide would tell her anyway, even if he knew. Which left her with no choice but to smile politely and make her way to the dining room, where—for all her supposed enthusiasm about eating breakfast—Emerald could do little more than disconsolately stir the pistachio-flecked yoghurt round and round in its little golden bowl.

Had Kostandin instructed his aide to be as obstructive as possible? she wondered bleakly. Suddenly it was difficult to keep her destructive thoughts at bay, because why had Luljeta's portrait made such an untimely appearance—had the King been gazing on it with nostalgia, perhaps?

She stared out of the window, where the roses dancing in the bright sunshine seemed to mock her suddenly deflated mood. Of *course* he had been feigning sleep last night—deep down she'd known that. She had sensed his instant retreat the moment he'd orgasmed. And there was her, imagining that it had been in some way special. How could it have been when he'd rushed away afterwards—creeping out some time in the night when she was still asleep?

Her throat grew dry as agitation prickled over her skin. Was this how he intended it to be, going forward? No real change in his behaviour at all? A scrap of affection offered here—and then instantly retracted, so she never knew whether she was coming or going.

What had she said to herself about being passive?

As she made her way back up the sweeping staircase, she was aware of having every kind of conceivable entertainment at her fingertips for the day ahead. Being here was like the ultimate five-star holiday, all expenses paid. She could swim in the pool, or walk around the beautiful grounds and take photos with her brand-new camera, or ring for someone to take her into Plavezero, but… Suddenly the prospect of any of those things felt so empty. Just as this place—this *palace*—felt empty. As if the heart had been ripped out of it, leaving nothing but a gaping hole behind.

Was that what had happened when Luljeta had left the marriage—had she left a broken man in her wake? He had explained that it had been a marriage of convenience but nobody had forced him into it, had they? It wasn't as if a son and heir had been driving his proposal, as it was with Emerald. Perhaps Kostandin had grown to love his beautiful queen along the way. Did that explain his often icy demeanour towards Emerald, and reluctance to take her to bed until last night? Until she had dressed up like some cut-price siren and practically dragged him there! But to *her* bed, she remembered bitterly, not his...

Her footsteps slowed as she passed Kostandin's chamber, unable to stop the cold serpent of curiosity from uncoiling inside her. She looked around but there was no sign of any servants and she wondered what she had been expecting. A couple of armed guards, standing sentry outside his room, perhaps? This was his *home*, for heaven's sake—even if right now it didn't feel like one. Her head still spinning with indecision, she came to a halt. She should walk straight past. But even as she thought it, her fingers were closing over the gilded handle and, pushing open the door, she quietly let herself inside.

For a moment she just stood there, acclimatising herself to the atmosphere of the vast salon. It was completely silent, all sound muffled by rich velvet drapes and heavy brocade, and it was much darker than the room she'd been given. Deep, masculine shades of red abounded, with exquisitely carved dark furniture and a rather menacing-looking sculpture in one corner. Her heart was crashing against her ribcage as she walked from the salon through to the bedroom, not really knowing what she was looking for.

Yes, you do.

You're seeking out the ghost of the woman who came before you.

But she found nothing to pin her fears onto. There were no photos or portraits of Luljeta in here. In fact, there was no evidence of a woman's touch at all in this dark and forbidding room. It was like a lavish version of one of the bedrooms at the Colonnade Club—completely anonymous, and soulless.

'What are you doing?'

The voice was icy and Emerald whirled round, the crashing of her heart intensifying when she saw Kostandin standing there. She hadn't heard him enter and as she met the quiet fury in his eyes, suddenly she was scared. Because there were unspoken rules when you lived in a palace and she had probably just broken the most fundamental of them all. You didn't enter the King's private bedchamber without invitation, even if he'd asked you to marry him. You were supposed to know your place. To sit back and admire all his kingly accomplishments and do whatever he or one of his aides suggested. The would-be bride auditioning for a role the King had no real stomach for, something which was becoming glaringly apparent. Emerald felt the familiar twist of pain in her heart. Even when he let her close, he ended up pushing her away—as if she were a toy he could play with, until he grew bored.

'I said, what are you doing?'

Somehow Emerald managed to meet the ice in his eyes without flinching. And maybe this was a conversation which couldn't have been started in any other way because, inevitably, he would have cut it short. She wasn't going to insult either of their intelligence by prevaricating and saying she'd wanted to see the colour of his drapes. Or behave like a burglar, caught in the act, even if his cutting blue gaze was making her feel that way.

'I wanted to see your bedroom.'

'Well, now you've seen it.'

'And? *And?*' She balled her hands into fists. 'Aren't you going to ask me why, or are you just not interested? No, I can see you're not. No change there, then!'

Kostandin tensed, sensing the showdown which was near and, though he loathed the kind of ugly exchange which was all too reminiscent of the atmosphere in which he'd been raised, maybe it would clear the air once and for all. And make her understand that boundaries really did mean boundaries.

'Tell me, then,' he drawled. 'If it makes you feel better.'

'Oh!' The fists were curling like claws against her yellow dress. 'Do you have any idea how patronising you can be at times? I wanted...' She sucked in a deep breath. 'I wanted to see if you had created some sort of shrine to Luljeta and if that was the reason why you didn't want to bring me here last night.'

'A shrine to Luljeta?' He furrowed his brows and the confusion in his voice sounded genuine. 'Why would I do something like that?'

'Because there's a damned portrait of her currently sitting in your aide's office!'

His mouth hardened. 'It was one of her favourite portraits, which she has requested be returned to her.'

'Oh.'

'But I should not need to explain my actions to you, Emerald,' he continued, his voice just as icy. 'And nor do I intend to. I do not need to answer to *you*.'

For a moment Emerald couldn't speak. She felt winded—as if the world had briefly become blurred, and when it came back into focus it looked like a different place. 'Even if I were prepared to overlook the sheer arrogance of that statement, I would still be left with the conclusion that a marriage between us isn't going to work.' She sucked in a shaky breath. 'I've tried to be understanding, Kostandin. I really have. Because you've had a difficult upbringing, which probably didn't encourage you to talk very much on a personal level—'

'Every cloud has a silver lining,' he interjected sardonically.

'Although I recognise that you've probably told me more than is usual for you.'

'So what's your beef?' he demanded.

'I know you only ever planned to have a one-night stand with me and that you've tried to do the right thing ever since—in that rather uptight way you've developed since the time I last saw you. And I suppose I must be grateful for that, because I'm certainly not without flaws myself. Who is? I came to Sofnantis with a view to moving here with Alek and making a real go of our marriage, but I don't…' She swallowed. 'I don't think I can live with a man who keeps shutting me out.'

'You think I was shutting you out last night?'

'I'm not talking about sex, Kostandin. You're brilliant at sex. You know that. But you didn't spend the night with me, did you? You weren't there when I woke up this morning and somehow I wasn't surprised.' She walked over to the window, the silk of her lemon dress rustling like the wind as she moved. 'Maybe you were just pre-serving decorum, because you're a king and didn't want to make the servants gossip because, as you pointed out yesterday, I don't have any real status.' She hesitated. 'So was your reluctance to spend the night with me gov-erned by the fact that we're not married? And will that change if or when we are?'

Kostandin tensed as a heavy silence followed her question. She looked so vulnerable right then that once again his heart began to ache with something he didn't understand, but he steeled himself against the flare of hope in her eyes. He would *not* engage with her at this level. Not now and not ever. Why give her the oppor-tunity to dissect him and pick him apart as women al-ways tried to do—to get inside his *head* and then spend the rest of her life messing with it? He would not give her that power.

'No, I'm afraid it will not,' he said eventually, trying to keep his words succinct and matter-of-fact. 'Let me try and explain to you why that is, since you obviously know little of royal life—'

'There you go—patronising me again!'

'Having separate bedrooms isn't considered unusual

for a monarch,' he continued calmly. 'It helps keep mystique and excitement alive—a benefit to any marriage, surely? Don't worry about it, Emerald. You'll soon get used to it.'

'There! You're doing it again,' she said. 'Deliberately pushing me away. I don't think keeping mystique and excitement alive is what's motivating you, Kostandin, as much as trying to avoid intimacy itself. You pretended to be asleep last night, didn't you? You didn't want to hear what I might want to say. Heaven forbid that I might start murmuring words of endearment.'

'That's enough,' he bit out.

'I don't think it is. Because I confess I'm perplexed. Sometimes you sound as if you're really angry with me and I just don't understand why. So what is it? What have I done that's so wrong? Is it because I didn't tell you that you were a father, even though I explained all the reasons why I kept it quiet? Is it because I'm a commoner and deep down you resent that? Or is it because I have the nerve to speak to you as a man, instead of as a symbol of greatness and power?'

A slow breath left Kostandin's lips. If knowledge was power, then didn't she already possess a large enough armoury which could be used against him at any time? But maybe he needed to say this if she wanted to understand him. It would help her accept why he could never be the man she might want him to be.

'I would no longer *be* King of Sofnantis,' he said savagely, 'if you hadn't brought the boy into my life.'

'What…what are you talking about?'

He shook his head impatiently. 'When I inherited

a crown I had never wanted, I saw it as a type of fire-fighting I needed to do to repair the damage done by my father and brother.'

'And you did a great job, by all accounts. The economy is booming and the people obviously love you.'

He waved away her attempt to placate him. 'But my attitude to being King didn't alter,' he continued remorselessly. 'It was still an unwanted burden and once Sofnantis had recovered economically, I was determined to address my own future. I was divorced by then. I had no plans to remarry and I certainly wasn't going to have children. And that was to be my freedom,' he emphasised.

'I still don't understand.'

'Don't you? Think about it, Emerald.' He gave a bitter laugh. 'Kings need a bloodline, and I never intended to have one. I had planned to abdicate to allow my cousin Namik to be King. He is next in line to the throne, a dutiful and clever man with a delightful wife and young son. He would have been perfect for the role. He still would. But that can never happen. Not now. Because one day you walked into my life and in the time it took for you to tell me about Alek, my world changed out of all recognition. He is the rightful heir and if I abdicate, Alek will lose out on his birthright. Not only that—but if I abdicate for personal reasons, it will weaken the monarchy and my conscience will not allow me to do that. Now do you understand?'

'Yes, I see,' she said slowly. 'But why do you hate being King so much? Especially when you're so good at it.'

He shook his head impatiently. 'Because I am trapped by the constraints of these gilded chains and by the total lack of freedom! By the way people look at me wherever I go, and listen to whatever I have to say, nodding their heads like obedient dogs at whatever springs from my mouth.' His eyes narrowed. 'Except for you, of course,' he added reflectively. 'You have never been quite so… obedient.'

'And this…this life of restraint—these gilded chains you speak of,' she said, her eyes narrowing. 'Is that what you wish for our son?'

'He needs to be given the choice,' he argued. 'Alek is heir to a great country and a great fortune and he deserves to know that. We cannot hide that knowledge from him, Emerald. Who knows how he might regard his future legacy? He might love it.'

'He might,' she said uncertainly.

Emerald's thoughts were buzzing as she tried to process everything he'd just told her. It explained a lot. The resentment and anger which simmered beneath all that red-hot desire and which had made him push her away so often. These were painful things to hear and she could easily react by showing him she was hurt. But at least he had been honest with her—and didn't she owe him a similar honesty in return?

She thought about the lifestyle and circumstances which had forged him. The unfaithful mother who had never loved him. The weak father and addict brother. She'd seen the anguish on his face when he'd talked about his past. Was it any surprise he'd never wanted to create a family of his own, with that as an example? And while he might be stern and angry at times, he was also brave. And strong. He hadn't wanted the crown but he had worn it well for the sake of his country, and now he was prepared to continue wearing it, for the sake of his son. He was prepared to change in a very practical way.

Couldn't she show him that emotional change was possible too, if only he would let his guard down enough to embrace it? Was she also capable of being strong— strong enough to swallow her pride and tell him how she really felt about him? Didn't a man whose mother had never loved him deserve some kind of acknowledgement that he wasn't an unlovable man?

She cleared her throat. 'You once asked me why I was a virgin when I met you, but I never told you, and maybe it's time I did. You see, after my mum got pregnant, she spent the rest of her life drumming it into me and Ruby that men were bad and you should never trust them.' She shrugged. 'And it doesn't seem to matter how balanced you try to be about relationships, when you reach adulthood some of that indoctrination is bound to sink in. So I was always really, really careful around men. I hardly ever went out on dates and when I did, I was just incredibly bored.' She paused. 'Maybe I sub- consciously chose boring men rather than men who did dangerous things to your pulse-rate, thinking they'd be safe. Until I met you.'

'And I was dangerous?' he surmised silkily.

'Of course you were.' She laughed. 'And I can see from your expression what you're probably thinking. You think I wanted you because you were a prince. That women only want you because you're rich and royal, blah-de-blah-de-blah. It has nothing to do with your intelligence or wit, or your knockout body and incredible blue eyes. Yet, despite your lofty position in life, you made me feel like we were equals—even though, patently, we weren't. I'd never thought it could be so easy to talk to a man and fancy him, all at the same time. When you made it clear there was no future for us, I accepted that, even if I didn't want to. If circumstances had been different I would have come to you and told you that you were a father and you now know why I didn't. But I never stopped thinking about you. How could I, when I saw your features in our son every day of my life?'

His mouth remained tight, his blue eyes cold. 'Why are you telling me all this, Emerald?'

It was right up there as contender for the most hurtful of responses to such an emotional declaration, but Emerald forced herself to continue, even though tears were pricking at the backs of her eyes. She had to stay resolute, to show him she meant every word, without scaring him off with the crazy truth. That she loved him. Her pulse thumped. That deep down, she had always loved him. Of course she had—why else had she put herself through all this? And just because he didn't feel the same way about her, that didn't mean it couldn't change. She swallowed. Because wasn't hope the bedrock of love?

'What if I tell you that I think we could be happy together as a family?' she suggested tentatively. 'If you could only stop putting up so many barriers to that happiness. If you could learn to trust us—and yourself. Alek is an affectionate little boy, who would love to shower some of that affection on his dad. Think how wonderful that could be, Kostandin. Because doesn't love give you its own kind of freedom? Our family could provide an escape from all the pomp and ceremony which surround you. It could be a place of real safety and refuge.'

'I think that's a little fanciful,' he answered coolly. 'So let's just keep our expectations real, shall we? I will do my best to be as good a father to Alek as I can, especially since I suspect you will have no qualms about telling me when I'm doing it wrong.' He allowed a flicker of humour to curve his lips, before his features assumed their familiar stony mask. 'To you I can offer affection, respect and fidelity and that will have to be enough. Because, frankly, that's all I have to give.'

She sensed he was making a big concession and maybe if it had been just her she might have accepted his terms, in the hope that he might soften his rigid stance over time. But it wasn't just about her. She had their son to consider and he had to be her number one priority. And even though the words were sticking in her throat like little pebbles, she forced herself to say them.

'I'm sorry, Kostandin, but it's not enough. I don't want a fixed-term contractual marriage, where emotion and love are out of bounds.'

'Are you holding out for romance, Emerald?' he questioned mockingly. 'Is that what this is all about?'

A lump rose in her throat and in that moment she hated him for his perception and yes, his cruelty. Of course she wanted romance. She wanted it all—but she was damned if she was going to let him know that. He might have ripped her heart to shreds, but no way was he going to destroy her self-respect.

'If I'd been holding out for romance I would never have gone with you in the first place!' she declared. 'Maybe you think being a royal means you don't have to make much effort because with you, it's all been terse instructions about what you will or will not tolerate—even on that very first time we slept together. Though at least back then you stayed the night.'

She stared down at the blurred pattern of the silk carpet, blinking her eyes once or twice, and when she lifted her gaze again, she was composed enough to be able to speak without her voice trembling. 'But it's made me realise that, not only do I owe it to our son to turn down your mean-spirited offer of carefully rationed affection and as little emotion as you can get away with, but I owe it to myself, too. Because he and I are worth more than that. Much more.'

'More than what?' he demanded.

'This! This fancy, empty palace of yours!' She sliced her hand wildly through the air. 'I don't want Alek growing up in an environment where he has to spend his time tiptoeing over eggshells in case he does or says the wrong thing. We may not have much in the way of possessions in our little house in Northumberland, but it's spilling over with love and nobody is afraid to express their feelings. I won't stop you seeing him, Kostandin. In fact, I'll make it as easy as possible for you, because that is the right thing to do. If you still want to abdicate, I'll be as discreet as you want. But that's none of

my business. I just want out of here. I want to go back
to England. I can't stay here in this atmosphere.'

She met his gaze, praying that the last trace of her
tears had vanished. 'I want to go home as soon as possible, and you can make that happen for me, Kostandin.
Please. Just set me free.'

CHAPTER FOURTEEN

KOSTANDIN PACED UP and down the long gallery, his long strides making short work of the lengthy dimensions of the gilded room.

How dared she?

How *dared* she?

Telling him what she would and wouldn't tolerate from their relationship! Listing a catalogue of complaints against him and then demanding he make his plane ready to have her flown to England as quickly as possible. Why, Emerald Baker was acting as if *she* were the royal and he her humble lackey!

He could have told her no, that she would have to wait until the morning for a scheduled flight leaving from Plavezero airport—and hadn't he been tempted to do that? As if by flexing his undoubted muscle and power he could punish her, as she had tried to punish him. But in the end he'd decided that this intolerable situation should not be extended any longer than it needed to be and had arranged to have his private jet on standby.

'Your Majesty?'

Impatiently, he glanced up as the doors to the first-floor gallery were opened. 'What is it, Lorenc?'

'Miss Baker is just about to leave for the airport and I wondered…' The aide gave a polite cough. 'Is His Majesty intending to bid her farewell?'

'No, His Majesty most definitely is not intending to bid her farewell,' he bit out. 'Have her gone. I have work to do.'

But once his aide had left, Kostandin found his footsteps automatically straying towards the window—though he took great care to stand to one side, making sure he was hidden from sight by the heavy drapes. The waiting car was gleaming, the royal flag fluttering in the light breeze as the chauffeur stood to attention. And then he saw her, walking down the short flight of marble steps, wearing… He frowned. Wearing the very jeans she'd arrived in, and carrying not just her computer case, but a small and very battered suitcase. He frowned again. Why were the servants not taking it from her? Why hadn't someone provided her with a decent set of luggage? And was she really leaving behind the expensive and updated wardrobe she had acquired since being here?

She looked up then, as if she sensed being watched, the expression on her heart-shaped face impossible to see, and Kostandin felt his heart contract with something which felt like pain as he saw the sunlight bouncing off her golden hair. But better the brief pain of parting than the enduring hurt of something he was fighting with every fibre of his being. He turned away from her distracting image, trying to get his tangled thoughts in order and wondering where they went from here. There were many things they needed to consider—his relationship with Alek, for a start, though that might best be done through professional mediators, once the heat of her departure had died down.

But the conflict raging inside his head showed no sign of abating during the next few days as he went about his busy schedule, trying to distract himself with the customary round of business delegations, receptions and dinners—though he was aware of slamming his office door more often than was usual.

He worked diligently on the routine piles of official papers but at times the words danced and blurred and he could feel the inexorable mount of frustration building inside him. His mind kept returning to Emerald and it didn't matter how hard he tried, he couldn't stop thinking about her.

He let out a heavy sigh as he pushed his pen away. Not just the obvious things—like her beauty or her sensuality, or that she had nurtured such a beautiful son. Her strength and resolve were equally admirable—for she had refused to be dazzled by the trappings of his position, hadn't she? She was willing to turn her back on them all because she wanted the best for Alek. She hadn't demanded money, or power, or an elevated position in society—all she had wanted was honesty and emotion and he had been unwilling and unable to provide them for her. At least he was free of her and her demands, he reasoned. A muscle began to work at his temple. So why the hell did he feel so…empty?

His thoughts were interrupted by a light tap on the

door—his barked reply enough to summon into the office Lorenc, who was carrying what looked like a photograph.

'What is it?' Kostandin questioned.

His aide carefully placed the photo on the desk in front of him. 'I was wondering if we might use this to accompany the press statement about your forthcoming trip to Maraban, Your Majesty.'

Kostandin was tempted to snap back that this kind of decision was way below his pay grade, when he glanced at the black and white shot and his heart missed a beat when he realised it was one of Emerald's. He had always been the first to acknowledge her talent but now he found himself picking it up to study the image more closely because... He swallowed. It didn't *look* like him. The stern and occasionally forbidding expression of his formal portraits was nowhere to be seen. His lips were curved in what appeared to be a failed bid to repress a rising laugh and his eyes were...soft... He shook his head in confusion.

As if he was looking at something which pleased him very much.

Or someone.

But he had. He had been looking at her.

Her.

The only woman who had ever been able to make him really smile. He stood up and went over to stare at the roses whose heady perfume was drifting in through the open French doors, and could feel his resistance crumbling. He found himself thinking how different the atmosphere in the palace had been when Emerald had been living there. For the first time the mighty citadel hadn't felt like a cold monument, or the symbol of a position he had never asked for—it had come *alive*.

And he had come alive, too—like a parched piece of ground being sprinkled with sweet water. He *liked* her company, he realised. Her feisty curiosity and stubbornness might have irritated him at times, but she always intrigued him. Her calm questions had made him examine himself in a way he'd never done before—and wasn't it better to confront the darkness she had exposed, than to bury it away again and let it moulder?

His throat dried. She hadn't flinched when he had laid out his unfeeling demands, telling her she must never love him, nor expect any real intimacy. He had implied that he would just carry on exactly as before and she and the boy would be expected to fit in around that. He had offered her marriage but that wasn't a marriage.

Not a real marriage.

He turned away from the sunshine, his head swimming, like someone emerging from a long sleep.

'Sit down, Lorenc,' he said slowly. 'I need you to help me make plans.'

Emerald glanced at her watch as she had been doing for the entire morning. She should be, if not happy, then at least a little bit glad. After all, it wasn't every week that you got two such well-paid jobs on exactly the same day, especially when you were a teeny organisation like hers and Ruby's. Her twin had been delighted to take a big batch of the local stottie cakes to some fancy hotel in Newcastle, where a famous footballer was revisiting his roots, while Emerald was on hand to deal with the somewhat mystifying request to book out their entire beach café for a private function.

She didn't even know how many people were supposed to be attending—in fact, she didn't know anything much at all. Her dealings had been with some posh-sounding woman in central London, who hadn't exactly been forthcoming. At least, the catering side of the booking was mercifully modest, which meant she was able to handle it on her own since the only food requested were two punnets of English strawberries, a tub of cream and some passion fruit. The customer would be providing their own booze as well as their own flowers.

Emerald blinked as she looked around. And what flowers they were. They had arrived in a fancy florist's van earlier. Stacks and stacks of fragrant roses in shades of deep crimson and faded lilac, their rich perfume filling the air. Dozens of blooms were crammed into exquisite crystal vases—which was a bit of a relief as otherwise they would have been destined to be displayed in a few hastily assembled jam jars.

But Emerald had been forced to fake her excitement, despite the jaw-dropping amount of money they were being paid for the gig. All she could think about was Kostandin and how much she missed him, even though she'd been trying her best *not* to miss him. But focussing on his arrogance and emotional rigidity was refusing to ease the terrible ache in her heart, which had been there since she'd left Sofnantis, almost a week ago. She had been evasive with Alek about her trip, she knew she had—but what was she supposed to say?

I'm sorry, darling. I've refused to marry your father because he won't ever be able to love me as much as I love him.

What had seemed to make perfect sense at the time now seemed like an act of complete selfishness—or was she just trying to talk herself into going back to him? And then what? Spend the next thirteen years of their contractual marriage wishing things could be different?

The flash of sunlight on an approaching car had her straightening her frilly apron, her official smile of welcome dying on her lips when she saw the identity of the tall figure who was unfolding his long limbs from the luxury vehicle. In his faded jeans and a T-shirt which matched the ebony gleam of his hair, he didn't look much like a king—especially not as he was carrying what looked like a cool bag. She screwed up her eyes, wondering if she was hallucinating. A *cool bag*? But her senses were so battered by his powerful presence as he walked into the café and closed the door behind him that any kind of rational analysis was proving impossible.

So she just stood there, surrounded by vases of scented flowers, trying not to show any heartache or regret on a face she hoped was composed—as befitted the mother of the King's child.

'Kostandin,' she said, her voice not quite as steady as she would have wished for. 'What on earth are you doing here?'

Kostandin put the bag on the floor wondering if she would comment on the chinking sound of glass against bottle, but she didn't. Hadn't she worked it out yet? But even if she had, it seemed she wasn't letting on and the

cool gaze she was directing at him from between narrowed green eyes didn't look particularly welcoming.

He was a man who had always been renowned for
his eloquence and articulation but for the first time in
his life, the words were sticking like glue in his throat.
Because how did you go about articulating something
you'd never said before? Something which experience
had made you wary of and you'd spent your whole life
avoiding? He swallowed. 'Because I want you to come
back.'

'Really?' She arched her eyebrows. 'Is this a power
thing?'

'To hell with power,' he said, unable to keep the desperation from his voice.

And then she clapped her palm against her forehead.
'Of course!' she exclaimed. 'It's all becoming clear now.
You're the mystery client who booked out the café.
Pretty extreme lengths to go to, aren't they? If you'd
picked up the phone, I would have agreed to a meeting.'

'But I didn't want a *meeting*,' he ground out. 'I wanted
to surprise you.'

'Well, you've certainly done that.' She slanted him a
look of defiance. 'The question is, why?'

'You made me realise I'd never shown you any romance,' he gritted out. 'And this is my attempt to make
up for that.'

'No, no. I get all that,' she said impatiently. 'But you
still haven't told me why.'

She wasn't making it easy for him, he realised. Did
she want him to jump through hoops of fire? 'Because
I need you, Emerald.'

But still there was no capitulation. Her mouth did not smile. 'Let's get this straight, Kostandin. It's not me you need.' She shook her head, as if to contradict the slight wobble of her voice. 'It's your son and heir. At least be honest—with yourself as well as me. I meant what I said about letting you see Alek as much as possible, but you'd better accept that I'm not coming back in order to secure your succession. I'm sorry, but I can't. I just can't.'

'This has nothing to do with succession,' he breathed urgently. 'And everything to do with you, and the way I feel about you, only I've just been too stupid and too stubborn to acknowledge it before.' She was shaking her head as he spoke, as if she wanted to block out his explanation, even though she had been the one who had just demanded it. 'You once told me that you never forgot me, well, as it happens, I never forgot you either, Emerald. After that first night we spent together, I couldn't get you out of my head. Or my body.' His jaw clenched. 'You wanted to know if there was a shrine to my ex-wife in my bedroom but you saw for yourself there was not. How could there be when she didn't spend a single night there?'

'Yes, you already explained that,' she said, in a bored tone. 'The King's precious bed is never shared with a woman.'

'No, it wasn't that. My marriage to Luljeta was unconsummated and was dissolved on those grounds.' There was a pause as he gazed into eyes which were now widening and he spoke the words slowly and very deliberately, for maximum impact. 'You are the only woman I've had sex with since that night in London, six years ago.'

'I'm not… I'm not sure I believe you,' she said, but a rush of colour had turned her cheeks rosy pink.

'Believe me,' he said roughly. 'Because it's true.'

'But… Luljeta is beautiful.'

'So what if she is? Do you imagine that a man is always controlled by his base instincts?' he demanded hotly. 'I didn't fancy her for all kinds of reasons and not just because she was my brother's fiancée and the thought of intimacy with her felt all wrong. And, just for the record, she didn't fancy me either. Because, by then I had met you and for me, that changed everything. You enchanted me, Emerald, and the spell you cast on me has never faded. Once the abdication had been made official, I had planned to come and find you, but then I happened to be in London and I didn't want to wait. I wondered if you were still working at the club. Why the hell do you think I held my party there when I had a whole embassy at my disposal? It was a long shot…' He paused. 'But there you were.'

'Let me guess.' Her voice took on an odd tone. 'You wanted to have sex with me to try and get me out of your system for good?'

'Perhaps that was what I thought would happen. I don't know.' He saw the way she bit her lip. 'You asked for honesty, Emerald, and that is what I'm giving you. Because when you came back to the embassy with me that night…' His throat thickened. 'It was like the culmination of all my recurring fantasies. Beautiful sex with the woman I'd been obsessed with. And then you told me about Alek. The discovery of a hidden heir gave me reason to mistrust you and I *wanted* that, because mistrusting felt safe. It was a situation I was comfortable with and certainly easier than the alternative, which was...' and now when he spoke it didn't sound like his voice at all '...to love you.'

Emerald sat in silence as his words rippled over her skin like velvet—words she'd never thought she'd hear him say, though she'd imagined them often enough, usually in her wildest dreams. But wasn't it strange how you could long for something and then be paralysed with fear when it came your way? As if she might still be dreaming. As if it might not be real. 'So where does that leave us?'

'I don't want a contractual marriage. I want a real one. Till death do us part. The whole deal. But I don't know how you'd feel about that.' He shrugged. 'Do I?'

She met his gaze, because surely the sincerity blazing from his sapphire eyes was too intense to be anything *but* real. But she needed to be sure. She needed to protect herself, for all their sakes. And, ironically, the only way she could do that was by opening up her heart and telling him how she felt. How she *really* felt.

'I love you, too,' she said slowly. 'I always have—even though I did everything in my power to try and stop myself. But even when you were being your most remote and objectionable, I never stopped loving you. Gosh, it's such a relief to be able to say it at last,' she admitted as he pulled her into his arms and her fingers began to stroke the dark rasp of his jaw.

'And such a relief to hear it,' he said, a deep note of

amusement curling his voice. 'Even though deep down I knew.'

'You're so arrogant, Kostandin.'

'Maybe,' he conceded. 'But would you have me any other way?'

'Ask me in a year's time.'

He kissed her then. A kiss which was long and hard and deep. A stamp of possession, but underpinned with a tenderness which tugged at her heartstrings, and when she finally came up for air, she could see that his eyes were as bright as her own.

'Oh, darling,' she said softly. 'Darling, darling, darling.'

'Tell me what you want, Emerald. And I will do everything in my power to give it to you.'

And suddenly it was so simple. As simple as breathing. Her finger was remarkably steady as it reached out to trace the outline of his beautiful lips. She didn't want the things he was capable of giving her. Not palaces, or planes or diamonds—because all those things were replaceable. But this wasn't, this feeling. And he wasn't, this man.

'You,' she said as his lips closed around her finger. 'That's all I want, Kostandin. You.'

EPILOGUE

'READ ME ANOTHER STORY, Papa—please!'

A pair of heavy-lidded eyes were turned upwards and as Kostandin met the gaze of a little boy who was valiantly fighting sleep, his heart turned over with love. 'No more tonight,' he said softly, planting a kiss on his head. 'You've had a busy day and we're going to have an even busier one tomorrow.'

Alek yawned. 'Can we go snorkelling again, Papa?'

'We sure can.'

'And will we see another turtle?'

'We might. But right now you need to go to sleep, young man, and I'm going to have dinner with your mama.'

A pair of dark eyelashes fluttered. 'Do you think she liked her birthday cake, Papa?' he murmured drowsily. 'Had you ever made a cake before?'

'Never,' said Kostandin with a smile. 'That's why it was so lopsided!'

Another quick kiss to the forehead, but the giggling boy was asleep before he'd even left the room and Kostandin just stood watching the soft rise and fall of his little chest before making his way across the terrace to the summer house that looked out over the cove below. Just like last year, they had spent the long vacation in their summer residence and, just like last year, he was happy. Happier than he had believed it was possible to be.

Deeply touched by a congratulatory message from Luljeta, he and Emerald had married in a low-key ceremony —she hadn't wanted comparisons made with his first marriage or to overwhelm their son with more pomp and ceremony than was necessary. But despite the dramatic change to all their lives, the three of them had quickly settled into what felt like unadulterated bliss. Kostandin had bonded with his little boy and had decided not to regret the past, but learn from it. They had become a family, he realised. A real family—not one riven apart by lies and deceit.

And Emerald had been right. Bonded by love as they were, the perceived chains which had bound him to the monarchy seemed to fall away. His position no longer felt like a burden and neither did his feelings. It was as if the woman he loved had shown him that it was okay to show your emotions, even if you'd spent the previous three decades pretending they didn't exist. Between them, they had created a modern royal family and tried to ensure that Alek had as normal an upbringing as possible.

He opened the door of the summer house and surveyed the interior with satisfaction, before dismissing the servant who had just finished lighting the final candle. And then he settled down to wait for her. Heard her light footfall before he saw her and, as always, his heart leapt.

'Kostandin?'

He didn't answer as she stood on the threshold, her filmy dress brushing against the curve of her belly, her hair gleaming in the flicker of the candle flames as she looked around, an expression of delight on her beautiful face.

'Kostandin,' she breathed. 'What is this?'

'Happy birthday, my love,' he said softly, then narrowed his eyes. 'Do you think it's over the top?'

Did she think it was over the top? Emerald wondered dazedly as she breathed in the rich scent of the roses which covered every available surface. Totally. There were white candles everywhere, little points of light glittering like so many indoor stars among all the flowers. At the far end of the summer house, which was relatively modest—one of the reasons she liked it so much—a table was laid for dinner, with a bottle of sparkling elderflower on ice—her favourite tipple throughout this pregnancy.

For a moment she was too choked to speak as her memory took her back to when she had agreed to become Kostandin's wife, and everything which had happened since then. These days he was no stranger to romance—indeed, he demonstrated it at every opportunity. That he was a considerate husband was in no doubt, but he was the most brilliant father, too. She'd watched the careful way he had taken time to bond with his son and relished his gentleness, which she suspected had never been given a chance to flourish before. Just as his kingship had flourished, his gratitude and happiness plain for all to see, making his people adore him even more.

The three of them had become a tight unit, and Alek was flourishing at the international school in Plavezero, while Emerald was rapidly learning how to make her adopted country proud of her. The language she was getting better at and her photos of Kostandin had been exhibited around the country to great acclaim and made into a book, with all the proceeds going to a charity for the homeless. She wanted to use her talent for good, she realised. She wanted to be a queen the King could be proud of.

Jessica had left and gone back to America and, to nobody's great surprise, Lorenc had resigned his post and taken up the Sofnantian ambassadorship in Washington DC. So far, there were no reports of a relationship.

Emerald's only sadness was Ruby's initial reaction to news of her marriage and that she and Alek were moving away from Northumberland. Her twin had explained how genuinely happy she was for her and then promptly burst into tears.

'I mean, I know you've got to go,' she had sobbed. 'But I'm going to miss Alek so much, Emmy. So very much.'

And Emerald had cried too, telling her beloved sister there would always be a place for her in Sofnantis and recognising that she'd been like a second mother to Alek and of course it was going to be hard to let that go. Ruby needed a family of her own, Emerald realised, and wondered whether that would ever happen.

She looked up to meet the loving and watchful gaze of her husband and went into his waiting arms. 'Only a bit over the top,' she said, with a giggle. 'You don't have to keep doing it, you know.'

'Ah, but I like doing it.' He kissed the tip of her nose and drifted his lips towards her cheek.

Emerald elevated her chin to allow him easier access to her neck. 'Don't get me wrong,' she breathed. 'I love all the romance, but it's all the other things you do which count more than anything. The way you nurture and care for me and do everything you can to ensure Alek and I are happy. The way you've cherished me throughout this pregnancy.'

He splayed his fingers over her bump and his voice was husky. 'I'm trying to make up for not having been there the first time round.'

'I know you are.' She touched her fingers to the side of his face, feeling so full of emotion that she thought she might burst. 'And that's one of the reasons why I love you.'

'Give me another reason,' he murmured as her fingertips began to tiptoe downwards.

'How about…*this*?'

Boldly, she reached for the erection which was pressing against his formal trousers and he gave a low laugh of pleasure as she began to stroke him with nimble fingers. And when it appeared that neither of them could wait much longer, he carried her over to the day bed and began to undress her—kissing every inch of the soft skin he revealed, as a silvery moon rose high over the Sofnantian sea.

* * * * *